HERITAGE

"What did you find out from this last book?"

"I'm not sure." She hesitated.

"Every time I read about those slaves packed and smothered on a slave ship, squashed together spoon-fashion, dying of disease, thirst, rat bite and not enough air, it made me want to hurt somebody."

Finally, she said, "You know something? With grand ancestors like those who came through the water watching ten million thrown overboard and survived the ship crossings from Africa, anyway, who knew about Mississippi lynchings, and lived on in spite of them . . . When I think about those folks, I think about staying around here a while . . . about living every moment of my life to its fullest . . . out of respect."

Other Avon Flare Books by
Joyce Carol Thomas

BRIGHT SHADOW
MARKED BY FIRE

WATER GIRL

JOYCE CAROL THOMAS

AN AVON FLARE BOOK

I thank Mitch Douglas, agent/believer

I thank Sharon Shavers, editor

WATER GIRL is an original publication of Avon Books. This work has never before appeared in book form.

AVON BOOKS
a divions of
The Hearst Corporation
105 Madison Avenue
New York, New York 10016

Published by arrangement with the author
Library of Congress Catalog Card Number: 83-90393
ISBN: 0-380-89532-3
RL: 6.5

First Avon Flare Printing: February 1986

Printed in the U.S.A.

K-R 10 9 8 7 6 5 4 3

For Aresa Pecot

amber: a reddish-brown jewel the color of mountains in Indian summer, a creation of resin from pine trees plunging long ago to the bottom of the sea, buried there for ages, collecting beauty till washed ashore by that ancient midwife Water

Thirst

ONE

Swish. Swish. The golden wings of an eagle whispered high above the back woods of Tracy, California.

Swish. Swish. The eagle lowered hushed wings. Peering down, he scanned the river where water sparkled like lace fringing the late-afternoon mountains.

At a bend in the river where two low hills covered with redwood and pine trees almost touched, the eagle spotted a figure swimming back and forth in an aqua-green bathing suit.

Swish!

He swooped closer, then glided just above a brown girl who moved through the lace-blue water as gracefully as a fish.

Tucking his wings to his sides, he dove down and dipped his beak into the river a few yards downstream.

He drank there until his thirst was slaked, all the while listening to the girl's splashing legs propelling her through the water toward the sloping shore.

She stepped out on the bank. The word *Amber* swirled, embroidered in blue thread across the aqua swimsuit top. She shook the water from her black lamb's wool hair until it sprayed onto her brown shoulders.

Then she walked toward the evergreen trees to change into blue jeans, her feet printing patterns on the dry land while fine particles of sand powdered her wet heels and toes.

As she changed clothes the eagle drew his claws up, threw his head back, shook his wings, and spread them like two golden fans opening in the California sunshine.

Then, soaring over peach orchards, asparagus fields the color of feathery ferns, and Tracy farmhouses with rooster weather vanes catching the light, he followed the barefoot Amber.

She approached a tomato patch of workers running up and down the rows, balancing lugs of red tomatoes on their heads, their long manly arms swinging in rhythm with their moving legs as they hurried to make another quarter. Every cent counted in their hustle to take money home to Mexico before the all too short harvest ended.

Slaving for below-minimum wages, the girl thought.

She passed close enough to see other workers, their backs bent like pretzels as they grabbed the red fruit loose from the prickly vines and shot them in the lugs they pulled alongside them like brown, rough-carved cradles. She saw grimy sweat puddling at the bottoms of their chins.

And the smell of hard work mingled with the hot tomato vines was so pungent, it stung her nose.

"*¡Hola!*" she called in greeting.

"*¿Qué pasa?*" they replied. Then to each other they hooted, "*¡Qué negrita bonita!*"

At her passing they began a mariachi song.

Coo coo roo coo coo cantaré. The sad sweet plaintive sound of Mexico streaked the air until she could almost see serapes, huaraches, piñatas, and guitars.

She looked into the Indian hatchet face of the last tomato picker and glimpsed not an exploited field worker but a flesh-and-bone sculpture of an Inca Indian transported to a Tracy, northern California tomato field. What time barriers had he crossed?

He lifted his full lug, brimming with tomatoes, straightened his back, and ran down the row with his burden. A map of water soaked his dusty worker's shirt in a trail that led from his neck to his waist.

When she passed him chalking his number on his tall stack of tomato boxes, he shook his sweaty sombrero loose from his coal-black head of curly hair and threw his head back and crooned, *"Coo coo roo coo coo cantaré, coo coo roo coo coo amaré."*

She walked on, the eagle shadowing her high above.

Swish whispered the eagle.

Soon she was walking down Corral Hollow Road.

The eagle followed her until she turned onto a grass path studded with fieldstone.

She stopped at the door of a redwood-shingled house shaded by chinaberry trees, turned the knob, and entered.

Dropping out of the sky, the bird looked like a moving sculpture of golden feathers. From his perch on the chinaberry branch, he looked through the dining room window covered with sheer white curtains, valenced at the top. Under the first curtain was another layer of sheers crisscrossed and tied with a ruffle of the same fragile material. Light falling through the curtains gave the room a serene softness.

The eagle saw a family seated at a round pine table, holding hands while the father said the blessing. The father, mother, and grandfather closed their eyes prayerfully, while two twin boys bowed their heads but peeked hungry eyes at a platter of smothered chicken.

Amber sat between the twins.

Behind her, the living room spread out like a page out of some homemaker's decorating magazine.

Amber's mother had scrubbed the oak floors until they gleamed like gold, until the seams in the parquet danced with light. A center rug embroidered with blue trumpet vines hooking themselves into a round wreath added warmth and comfort. The mother had rinsed the enormous plate-glass window in vinegar water and shined it with a soft lintless rag until one wondered whether or not there really was any glass in the pane. Amber often looked out this window to capture a panoramic view of the sea. It was a simple room, sparsely furnished but alive with light and warmth.

A rocking chair sat next to a little wicker table. When Amber was much younger, her father would rock her to sleep here. A couch, upholstered in a fabric woven from blue and red threads, sat opposite the rocker. Before her father would rock her to sleep, her mother would tell her stories on this couch. From a distance the blue and red threads gave off the color of purple. It was only when Amber was closer, sitting on the couch in her mother's lap, sucking on her three middle fingers and listening to the story of the bear who went fishing in a lake, that she could see where the red stopped and the blue began.

Two straight-backed oak chairs and a music stand centered in front of the oak chairs sat off in the bright corner near the plate-glass window.

Over the brick fireplace, guns, oiled and shined, gleamed down like trophies. On either side of the fireplace along the entire length of the wall was a gallery of black-and-white pictures in oval oak frames, encased in glass—grandparents on her mother's and father's sides. Ancient aunts and uncles. And largest of these ovals was a family portrait. Her mother in a Sunday white blouse and light frilled jacket; her father in a

Sunday white shirt and linen suit; her twin brothers, one on each side, dressed in Easter outfits, Amber in the middle, a fantastic ribbon crowning her head, her hair lovingly parted into tiny plaits braided so neatly, so tightly into little pigtails, it hurt to grin. That's why she looked so somber and stern-faced. Everybody else was smiling. She was the only one different, looking solemn.

Now, at the dining room table, she was again looking solemn, sitting between her two younger brothers, the twelve-year-old twins, tall and skinny as two cattails down by Bear River.

While the blessing was going on, Amber's eyes were respectfully closed, her mouth frowning.

"Amen," said her father. David Westbrook immediately rubbed his pouch of a stomach at the sight of the food. David had a balding spot on the very top of his head that you didn't notice until he bowed his head to pray or read. His plumbing customers noticed it when he was on the floor repairing their kitchen sinks.

"Out swimming again?" Jason, one twin, said to Amber.

Twelve-year-old Johnny, still smarting from the beating she'd given them in the swim race the day before, added, "Mama and Daddy found you in a pond."

"Is that why I'm the oldest?"

"What do you mean?"

"Obviously they chose the mermaid before they got to the frogs."

"She called me a frog!" said Johnny, looking for sympathy.

He didn't get any.

The twins were always teasing Amber about being different.

Their mother and father exchanged glances. This

was the age-old game all brothers and sisters played on each other. Wanting to be the only one in the family, a brother or sister pretended that another child had been found in a pasture or in a frog pond.

She continued, "Coming back from the river I passed the farm workers," Amber said. "It's a shame." And she began to list the ways in which the workers were taken advantage of.

"Is that so?" David Westbrook said, lifting his napkin and placing it on his lap.

Jason and Johnny mischievously mimicked their father's gesture but with more flourish than he managed, while continuing to eye the main dish.

"Have you seen the places those migrant workers have to live in?" Amber asked.

"Well, I don't suppose it's the Hyatt Regency or the Hilton."

"I'm serious," Amber said, getting heated up. "Not much better than a barn. I don't even think they sleep on sheets."

"I never get called to repair any sinks or showers out there. None of the other plumbers do, either. That tells you they don't have any indoor plumbing for those poor people. So I don't doubt your word, Amber," said her father.

"She's done her research, all right," said one of the twins, eyes still glued to the food.

On the other side of David, Grandfather Westbrook, fondly called Papa Westbrook, served himself a helping of mustard greens. A gray beard hid his chin. He leaned his thickly gray-haired head over and inhaled the tangy aroma of the greens and nodded his approval. "What did you see at the river today, Amber?"

"A golden eagle," Amber said. "But listen to this . . ." And she went on, chattering her complaints.

Papa Westbrook stared out the window. The skin around his eyes pleated into fans. Did his nearsighted eyes see the shadow of eagle wings flutter and rise above the chinaberries?

While Johnny scooped a mound of rice on his plate and Jason reached for the cornbread, Amber picked up the platter of chicken just in front of her.

The twins sighed, dismayed. Amber kept right on talking about the world's problems. She gestured with one hand while the other held the chicken captive.

"Please," said Johnny, looking at the chicken.

"Right," she said as she scooped up a drumstick. On the other side of her Jason groaned. He had wanted a drumstick, and since Johnny had his hand stuck out, he didn't have a chance.

"What I want to know is, how can people be so stupid as to continue to kill one another?" Amber asked.

"Doesn't your head get tired trying to figure all this out?" asked Jason, still yearning for the chicken. Finally he gave up, saying, "You're not our sister. They discovered you in the woods. Some owls raised you, that's why you're so curious," said Jason.

"Owls?" said Amber.

" 'Who'? Isn't that what owls are always saying?" said Jason, hoping she'd hand him the platter.

"I can think of a lot worse things to be than a bird," said Amber.

"Such as?"

"A jackass."

"Amber!" said Grace, exasperated.

"It's just an animal, Mama," said Amber with a grin.

"Please, please, please pass the chicken," said Johnny, still waiting with outstretched hands. "My aching arms are getting awfully tired."

She handed it over.

"A golden eagle, you say? Didn't we see one just before that last earthquake?" asked Papa Westbrook.

"Yes," said Amber, and kept on talking about cruelty.

Grace, a picture of neat plumpness, a woman the color of gingerbread, shook her head. She used to say about Amber, in order to explain that her daughter had always been a most curious child: "When she was a baby, she stared into the mouths of old men until they told their oldest secrets." Now she said, "Eat, Amber, while your food's hot."

Soup had been known to get cold and chicken to turn into brown jelly when Amber started on one of her long, long monologues, supporting her arguments with statistics delivered between bites of bread and swallows of hot chocolate.

Her flashes of sincere outrage lit up her eyes and deepened the dimples at the corners of her mouth, always reminding Grace of that innocent beauty that could come and go so suddenly, startling her every time she saw it.

"You're just scared of being ignorant," Jason said, pointing a fork at Amber. "Always showing off what you know."

Amber shrugged and started eating.

" 'Fraid it's just that colored curiosity that can't be quenched," said Johnny.

"I'm curious about this," said Jason, "how come I can't get a drumstick sometimes," just as Amber bit into the juicy meat.

Papa Westbrook nodded his head, stroked his beard, and smiled.

David looked at his daughter and said, "Pass the corn bread."

Grace reminded Amber, "Only problem is, the more you read, the more you need to know."

''Small problem. I read *Jet* and *Ebony,* and we talk enough about being Black, this is just more of the same, except it's other folks too,'' said Amber, setting her fork down so she could start chattering again.

''No, it's not the owl family that abandoned her, it was a mess of squirrels. She's off and chattering again!'' said Jason.

Grace cleared the table of dinner plates and served the dessert. The twins watched amazed as Amber's vanilla ice cream, at first sitting so proudly atop the peach cobbler, melted and ran on down the sides of the crust as she continued talking. The crunchy cobbler was flooded with cream until it was overwhelmed, soggy with disgrace. David finally stopped her with a request.

''Amber, I want you and Wade to play a duet for us after dinner. Saw Wade when I was driving up this evening. Invited him over.''

''But, Daddy, I was going to read,'' Amber complained.

''It *was* you who asked me if you could keep company with Wade Dewberry after you turned fifteen, wasn't it? Now you're telling me two months into fifteen that you don't want to be bothered?''

'' 'Course I do,'' she said, thinking of handsome Wade and his magnetic eyes, his powerful muscles. ''It's just that I have some reading.''

Every eye was on her, and she knew it was not only Wade they were thinking about but also music.

After dinner they heard Wade's light scratch on the screen door. And there he was with his husky self, almost taking up the entire door frame. A champion wrestler who played cello.

Papa Westbrook sat in his rocker by the living room window. The twins lounged on the blue hooked rug in the middle of the floor. David and Grace sat on the almost purple couch in the background, holding hands like teenaged lovers, much to the mortification of the twins.

Then all was silence as the duet began. Amber sat with her back straight, then leaned over the flute and began the introduction to "Sacred Mountain, Sacred Tree, Sacred River that Runs to the Sea," her cinnamon-colored lips soft and serious. She bowed her head over the flute and trilled until the music glistened.

Wade, astraddle the cello, began his part slowly, moving the cello bow into the melody, rising in swells, "Sacred Mountain, Sacred Tree, Sacred River that Runs to the Sea."

Then there was a moment between beats, a moment of perfect silence when power gathered. So strong that it touched Papa Westbrook and locked its fire in his arthritic bones. He found it difficult to sit still, so he rapped his cane against the floor.

"Play, children," he admonished.

To this audience Amber and Wade became a duet of one, their music two waterfalls flowing into one stream. They played for the family. They played for themselves. They played for Music. When Amber puckered her lips and made the flute sing, Papa Westbrook saw a trembling bird dip into the mountainside and shake a lone bush branch for berries.

When she played, she sounded like someone searching for some wonderful and awful secret, something she needed to know and which no one would tell her.

Then Wade lifted his head from the cello, scooped up the wind in his vibrato fingers. A river flowed beneath Papa Westbrook's feet. The twins caught their breath.

Papa wanted to change his walking cane into a fiddle or a trumpet, some instrument, but all he could do was strike it against the floor in appreciation.

At last the notes rose to a crescendo and reached their final resting place.

"Don't know if I could have stood anymore," said Papa.

The group of them chuckled.

After a while Wade asked, "Where's Amber?"

"Disappeared on us again," said Johnny.

"I swear she's got some haint in her," said Jason.

"She's reading; remember she said she had some book to finish," Papa explained.

"Amber," called Wade as he hurried down the hall after her.

He jingled the little brass deer knocker on her bedroom door.

She opened the door.

"Now you see her, now you don't," he piped.

She laughed, the flute in both hands.

"Can we talk soon?" he asked.

"Yes. Soon," she agreed, one hand on the doorknob, torn between talking to him and going to finish her book.

"I miss you," he said, gently moving her hand from the knob and encircling her in his arms. He kissed her.

"And I miss talking with you, I miss your kisses," she whispered.

She felt his solid strength flow down her spine and into her toes. As rough as he could be with an opponent in a wrestling match, that's how gentle he was with her.

She could stay this way in the circle of his tender embrace forever.

When they separated, she gave him that passionate look. A light in her eyes.

"You know, I don't know any other girl who can do that."

"What?"

"Turn the light on the way you do when you look at me."

"I didn't know . . ."

"Now you do. It's there deep in your eyes, and the only time I notice you turn it on is when you look at me."

"Well, you are a little special to me," she teased.

"The kind of chemistry they don't mention in the chemistry class. We've got it," he said.

"I do miss spending more time with you," she said. "Want to go hunting tomorrow?"

"It's a deal. And when you're finished with that book, I want to hear about everything you're reading."

The soft jangle of the door chimes held her for a moment as he closed the door to her room.

It was a room of rich woods, rose wall paper with raised rose petals and rose leaves, and pink muslin curtains. The miniature brass knocker on her door with its little brass wind chimes of prancing deer could be gently jingled until the deer danced, her mother's musical way of waking her in the morning or letting her know she was coming into the room.

One of Amber's earliest memories was of watching her mother shine and clean the chimes.

"Make the deer dance! Make the deer dance!" she had shrieked from the crib as her mother rubbed the brass with a soft cloth.

"Anybody who can talk that well is ready for a more mature bed," Grace told David.

"Well, it can't be just any bed. It's got to be fit for a princess."

And they took her looking in furniture stores, but nothing would please them. Nothing would do. They spent all morning looking.

That afternoon, when they stopped by Dr. Goldberg's for Amber's routine checkup, he had told them about a man who built furniture.

"From scratch?" asked Grace.

"Tell him what you want. I'm sure he can please you," said Dr. Goldberg, lifting Amber down from the examination table. "A clean bill of health."

David had written down the number and called up the furniture builder.

"We want a bedroom suite for our daughter, but we want it to be different. . . . What's she like?" David repeated back into the phone, winking at Amber. "She's a beauty, she likes the out of doors, she likes the ocean. . . . What size room? The room is a small one, well, not too small. Cozy. About ten by twelve feet. . . . Windows? Yes. Lots of light. Windows on two of the walls. . . . How soon can we see the plans? . . . That long? Well, quality takes time. You come highly recommended, Mr. Lockhart. Very well, sir, good-bye."

And they waited. And waited and waited.

"How long has it been, David?" Grace complained one day. "This child's getting so big, her feet are sticking out of the crib slats!" she added, exaggerating.

Then, the next day, Mr. Lockhart, the furniture builder, came by with the plans. Mr. Lockhart, a giant man in workman's denim coveralls. Skin the color of uncreamed coffee. Six feet six, hands like hammers. A laugh like a trombone.

"Is this the princess?" he asked, looking down at Amber.

"The one and only," said David.

"Well, now." He unraveled the plans on the dining room table and stood back. Amber remembered the rustling sound of paper, the smell of blueprints. He was a man of few words. His work spoke for him.

"Oh, look. Come here, precious," David called to Amber, delighted with the plans on paper.

"Color. Color," Amber cried, clapping her hands together, wanting to color the bed, whose headboard was a forest scene of bears and trees, a footboard of fish leaping from a water scene. Across from the bed Mr. Lockhart had sketched an oval-mirrored dresser with oak drawers carved in raised flowers. And next to it a chest of drawers with the three scenes of the bed and dresser repeated: the forest scene repeated on the top drawer, the raised flowers engraved on the middle drawer, and water jumping with fish on the bottom drawer.

Lockhart, the artist-workman, beamed.

"Oh, Mr. Lockhart, Mr. Lockhart," Grace said approvingly.

"Why, it'll be ready in another month," he promised, a gleam in his dark eyes as he smiled at Amber, "for the princess of Corral Hollow Road."

Then he bent over and handed Amber an extra copy of the plans, and she lay on the trumpet vine rug and colored in the furniture with crayons using the colors of bears, water, trees, fish, and sky while Grace served David and Mr. Lockhart little sour cream cakes and coffee.

Now in her room, filled with its original forest scene furniture, its one-of-a-kind design with the carved oak panels telling visual fairy tales, stories without written words, she listened to Wade's steps leading back to her family in the living room. Then she placed the flute on the music stand by the oval-mirrored dresser and turned immediately to her latest pile of library books.

TWO

The next morning Amber woke up at dawn. She bounded out of bed and started pulling on her clothes. It was time to go hunting with Wade and her brothers. Dressed as she was in her costume of hunting boots, jeans, yellow parka, knit cap pulled snugly over her ears, a shotgun slung across her shoulders, she looked like she could live up to her reputation as a master markswoman.

Always the first one up in the morning, she took the lead. "Time to go!" she yelled to her brothers. They jumped up out of their beds and into their hunting clothes and gear.

Johnny said to Wade as the wrestler bounced out of his front door in response to Amber's calling, "How do you like being bossed by a woman?"

"Depends on the woman," Wade said with a grin.

Jason nodded to that; obviously the champion wrestler on the Tracy High wrestling team was no cream puff.

"How can she lead me around by her apron strings? Look at her, she won't even wear an apron," Wade explained.

Grace, still in bed, glimpsed out the window at Amber dressed for hunting and she thought about her mother-in-law, Bonnie, who could shoot a hole through a nickel slug at ten paces. And Amber was as good a shot as Grace's mother-in-law had ever been.

"Just look at our daughter, David," she said nudging her husband awake.

David took one look, grinned, and fell back asleep.

This hunting day, Amber heard the lusty crowing of the bowlegged roosters as she and her brothers and Wade trampled through the fresh morning countryside, the dew wetting their boots.

They were on a rabbit hunt this glorious dawn.

Amber spotted the rabbit first. "Look!" And they stretched out like galloping greyhounds, graceful but deadly, and they wailed an attack howl that stripped the limbs from the trees and laced morning fear in the quick legs of the rabbit.

She propped the shotgun on her shoulder. Her slender but strong fingers pulled the trigger. The rough bullet whizzed by the rabbit's twitching nose.

He ran into a hollow sycamore. The nervous birds watched from dawn branches and camouflaged their trembling with puffed feathers. Nothing living was equal to the hot wildness of bullets. The cottontail scrambled out of the other side of the sycamore and stretched out across the field.

Amber ran after him, her braid unraveling, the curl of her hair tangled in the wind. Her boots struck brutally against the earth as she ran. Her knuckles tensed as she clenched her gun. Her face set like female granite.

Wade and the twins ran beside her.

The dry brush swam greenish-gray before their eyes as they wove through the sage and tumbleweed. They ran, the thrill of the chase charting their paths. The hot blood pumped faster through their veins as they propped their shotgun butts against their shoulders, aimed, and made their mark.

And the quivering rabbit lost the race with the bullet. Downed. The surrendered blood of the bunny pulsed into the ground, staining it as red as tomatoes.

The dawn was fully realized. And the sky was a pale bandage of blue cloth. A feeble, washed sun limped over the horizon and sprinkled subdued light across their faces as they studied the rabbit.

Back at the house, Amber yelled, "Hey, Mama!" as they slammed the door behind them. "We caught you a rabbit for dinner. Rabbit thought he could outrun lead, but we got him," she said. "Take a look at this," and Amber dangled the catch by one long furry ear.

She looked up expecting to see what? Pride? But what she saw was a shudder in her mother's eyes and the fleeting vision of a death squad: Amber, Johnny, Jason, and Wade all lined up in formation with their guns aimed at the helpless rabbit blindfolded and up against the wall of a tree trunk.

"Who got him?" Grace asked, a faint hoarseness to her words.

"Who knows?" Johnny shrugged. "We were all shooting at the same time."

Amber had nothing more to say. She just kept staring at her mother's eyes. Moonstones reflecting strange lights. But when her mother looked at her, she looked away.

"Will you dress the rabbit and cook him for dinner, Amber?"

"Yes."

Amber spread the rabbit out on newspaper on the kitchen table. Found the poisoned slugs and extracted them.

She skinned the rabbit, dug out his insides, cut him in two with the precision of a skilled surgeon. He dressed out to be three pounds. She prepared him with sage, salt, rosemary, and cayenne.

Next she chopped tomatoes and sprinkled them around his proud chest, split in half. Across his quick legs, soon to be succulent drumsticks, she spread minced bell peppers, red onions, celery, and thyme. Time. Time had run out for this creature of the wind.

She placed the rabbit in the Dutch oven to marinate in the savory spices until she cooked it for dinner.

All morning it marinated. Soon it was noon, and Amber's thoughts kept jumping back to the hunt. To take her mind off the new disturbing thoughts about the death-squad execution of the rabbit, she went into her room and picked up her flute.

The mellow call of the flute drifted on the air and trembled. Her fingers moved like a sure wind, at times joyful, mixed with honeyed sunlight like a rabbit running free on the hillside and at other times as melancholy as a gray dawn or a snared prey yearning to be free.

Through the window as she played, she could see Grace bent over her plants, tending her clusters of small purplish lavender, a living brooch on the bosom of her lavender-colored dress. And when the plant was not in season, she wore tiny dried blossoms. The gentle fragrance encircled her like an invisible haze. The words *Grace* and *lavender* would always mean gentleness to Amber.

Her flute playing finished, she went into the kitchen and peeked into the roasting pan in the oven. The delicious smell of the marinade drifted up, tickling her nose.

Through the kitchen window she saw Wade coming across the road, his back pocket stuffed with a strip of blue.

She met him at the door.

"Want to go swimming?" he asked.

"Sure. Wait while I get my suit." She fetched her swimsuit and headed for the door.

"Where're you going, Amber?" Grace called from the flower garden in the backyard.

"Swimming, Mama."

"No, ma'am. You will not go by yourself. Snakes are out there, Amber."

"Wade's with me."

"All right, then."

They struck out across the meadow, not saying much, just holding hands, listening mostly to the hum of the insects, enjoying the feel of the ground under their bare feet.

Soon they had reached the river.

As they stepped from behind their separate dressing trees, she challenged him, "Beat you to the other side?" And they raced the rest of the way to the river's edge.

She dived in and stroked her way across swiftly.

"Beat by a girl! But they did say you came here swimming, you ought to join the Tracy swim team. They need you."

"They couldn't take it. The girls are already jealous because you're my boyfriend. I hear them whispering behind my back. 'I don't know what Wade sees in her. She's cute, but she never wears fingernail polish. And look at that head. Obviously she spends zero hours on it. The Tracy High wrestling champion needs himself a queen. Now, take me for instance.' " And they both laughed at her mimicry of the envious girls.

"Pay them no mind. If you want to join the swim team, join."

"Well, maybe sometime. Not now. I'd rather enjoy my private victories with you."

They swam some more, then rested.

"You look just like a brown jewel," he said as they lay on the grass, letting the sun dry the beads of water still clinging to them. "I do believe you're half girl, half fish. And if you get any darker, you'll be a molasses mermaid."

"If I hide my feet in the grass, we could pretend they're fins." She giggled.

On the way home they kicked up rocks and ran and romped like jackrabbits.

At the house she stuck the marinated rabbit in the oven, prepared rice, took the rabbit giblets, and made rabbit gravy. "You're staying for dinner, aren't you, Wade?"

He nodded.

"Then do you want to make your famous salad?"

He made a lettuce and cucumber salad, sprinkled with dill weed, dressed with sour cream.

When the table was set, she rang the dinner bell.

Through the family chatter of day's events and crisp salad and flaky rice, the entire table of people seemed to pause a moment when they passed a forkful of the aromatic pepper-sweet rabbit to their mouths.

Delicious.

But they all had sense enough to eat with a studied humility.

Amber kept thinking about the rabbit and about the people in the books she read. Do animals belong to the cycle of cruelty, just as people, she wondered.

Soon Wade winked at Amber and said it was time for him to leave. They excused themselves from the table and went out into the evening air. Holding hands, they walked over to the chinaberry tree and stood beneath it. Then Amber turned to face Wade, a shy light glowing in her eyes. They hugged with such tenderness that they did not want to stop touching. Wade covered Amber's mouth with his until a delicious fire spread through their lips. The more they kissed, the more they wanted to—but when the first star winked at them, they said goodnight and went their separate ways into their own houses.

THREE

The next day Grace's words were still ringing in Amber's head: "The more you read, the more you need to know."

Her mother had been so right, she thought as she sat at the dresser braiding her hair, impatient to get to her books. This reading was getting to be addictive. She couldn't wait to read what happened next. If it was left up to her, she'd leave her hair standing all over her head. At least that's what Grace claimed. Sometimes Amber was forgetful of herself.

She was trying to read a book on the Japanese concentration camps and braid her hair at the same time.

"I need three hands!"

The scratch on the screen door. "Wade." She had asked Wade to go with her to Susie Yamashita's house.

Instead of finishing the braid—she had about two inches left to go—she threw a rubber band around the frizzly ends and rushed to the door.

"Ready?" he asked.

"They took old folks, babies, everybody with black straight hair and Japanese surnames and threw them behind barbed wire fences," she told Wade as they passed the tomato patch, the wheat field, the statues of hay waiting to be stored in the barn. "Locked them up like pigs in a pigpen."

"You're telling me? I gave you the book," said Wade.

She went on reciting. He let her, knew she had to get it out of her system. By the time she had finished her report, they had crossed through the south end of the Yamashita farm and come out near the front yard of the ranch house.

Japanese gardening with little shrubs and cypresses graced the front yard.

Susie, in a red blouse and blue jeans, waved to them from the front window and soon came skipping out in her sneakers and red socks and big grin to welcome them.

As usual they sat on the redwood steps, with the green junipers potted in redwood planters surrounding them. After talking about the latest song on the radio and the newest dance step, Amber expressed her concern about the Japanese concentration camps.

"Is it true they sent your family off to camps at the start of the Second World War?" Amber asked Susie.

"Yes," said Susie, and she lowered her short lashes.

"Tell me about it."

Susie shrugged her shoulders and blinked her almond eyes.

"Well, where did your family stay?" Wade asked.

Susie blushed. "They were herded to a place without heat in the winter, a place dirty with dust in the summer, given bad food and sometimes no indoor toilets." She swept her bangs and the anger out of her eyes. Changing the subject she said, "Hey, would you guys like some sushi? Mom just made some."

Amber ate the soy-sauced rice, ginger root slivers, and golden eggs wrapped in seaweed. She tried to swallow her curiosity with the food but ended up with a lump in her throat.

On the way home she said to Wade, "Why didn't she tell us more about those concentration camps?" She kicked a stone so ferociously, it landed several feet ahead of them.

"You're not mad at Susie. You're bothered because it happened."

"Oh, Wade," she whispered, "why is the world so cruel sometimes?"

She began reading the history of the Jews in Germany, Poland, and other parts of Europe. She dared not believe all the sadistic atrocities. They were enough to make her turn her back on the human race. Were they just words with nothing behind them?

"I've got an appointment with Dr. Goldberg this morning," she said to Grace as she vacuumed the round rug in the living room.

"What?" said Grace, who couldn't hear clearly above the vacuum motor. She was busy in the kitchen baking Amber's favorite dessert, peach cobbler.

"I said I have an appointment with the doctor."

Grace rushed into the room and turned off the vacuum motor. "Are you ill?" She felt Amber's brow for signs of fever.

"No, I just have to ask him about something I read in this book about the Holocaust."

"Are you sure that's all you want to ask him?"

"What else?" asked Amber.

"Of course, nothing else," said Grace uncomfortably.

Guess she doesn't like my prying, thought Amber as she put the vacuum cleaner away.

Book in hand, she walked briskly down Corral Hollow Road and turned on Grant Lane. She was so occupied with her thoughts that she did not see the jewel weeds bursting open, showing off their yellow colors when she brushed against them with her pant legs. She took for granted the perfume of wild honeysuckle and the Tracy sky of puffed clouds on clear blue. She kept walking until she came into town and to the Goldberg house.

"I wonder if you'd explain something to me," said Amber, settling herself into the curve of the sofa.

For a moment he looked uncomfortable, but the more she talked, the more interested he became. He answered her questions. Then, finally, he rolled up his sleeves and showed her a blue number tattooed along his arm. Here was living proof.

When she came back to Corral Hollow Road, she went straight to Wade's house and rapped on his door.

When he let her in, she plopped down, out of breath, as though she had been running a long race.

"Wade," she said, "It's true. They murdered over six million Jews. Six million people. Lined them up and marched them to the gas chambers. Teenagers and grandpapas and little boys and girls no bigger than the Reyes children down the road. Do you know that?"

"But, Amber, you took the book off my library shelf, remember?"

She went on, "Mouths mined for gold and made into jewelry for sale. Skins of murdered people used for lamp shades. They did experiments on women." These last words lashed out at him, and her voice began to rise even higher until he could feel it trembling.

"Well, here's your book back," she snapped, tossing it down so roughly, it tumbled off the edge of the coffee table and onto the floor.

"Amber, the book's not to blame. Anyway, much as you love books, what are you doing throwing one? Girl, have you gone and lost your mind?"

She bent over and picked it up. "I know the book's not to blame," she whispered apologetically and fled home, the door slamming shut behind her. She was always mortified when she became so overwrought and her anger appeared as rudeness.

That evening the flute was silent.

The next week, standing outside under one of the palm trees lining the Tracy High driveway where the students who lived in the country caught the bus home, Wade spied the title on the spine of Amber's latest book. Above the library numbers he read *Before the Mayflower*, a book of Black history.

A few days later, standing in his window, he saw Amber marching across the road to his house with the history volume in her hand. "Uh-oh, she must have turned the last page in that book."

"If I could, I'd give up reading, it's too darn upsetting!"

"Why don't you?"

"Might as well change my personality. You know I'm too curious. Speaking of being curious, what about your family? I know about the ongoing struggles of all Black folks from reading *Jet* and *Ebony* magazines. I know my own family history, but it occurred to me that I don't know yours."

"Where would you like me to start?" he said.

"With the Dewberry family."

"Oh, like every family we know, I suppose, my folks came from the South. But they came before I was born. So I'm first-generation Californian, the same as you. You just finished the book, you ought to be overflowing with answers by now. What about your family? How do they fit in with the story in that book?" And he folded his arms across his chest.

She began, "On my father's side the first recollection—written recollection—is of my great-great-grandmother slaving for a family called the Westbrooks. They tried to separate my great-great-grandfather from his wife and children. He killed the slave master and was chased across the country by a Ku Klux Klan posse. They didn't count on my female ancestor being an expert with a gun.'' Amber's imagination soared as she pictured the scene for Wade.

" 'The nigger's got a gun,' one night rider shouted as bullets zinged through the air. They said the Klansman lay so close to his horse, it looked as if he were trying to get inside the animal's skin. Trying to hide under the horse's hide,'' Amber said.

''When that didn't work, he tried to see which way the bullets were coming; when he did, he hollered 'The nigger's woman! It's the nigger's woman shooting!'

''She hit the bull's-eye. The grand dragon,'' Amber said.

''How many did they get?'' Wade wondered.

''Oh, I forget the exact number. But who knows? Who had time to count? In spite of their courage, Westbrook was injured fleeing Mississippi.''

''How was he hurt?'' Wade asked.

''Seems one eye was half shot out of his head. With one hand on the reins and the other holding his dangling eye, they rode on into Oklahoma,'' Amber said.

''Why Oklahoma?'' Wade wondered.

''I'm not sure. Probably the prospect of owning their own land. When the government bought land from the Indians, they offered millions of acres to non-Indian settlers who ended up running for the land in the great Oklahoma land rushes.

''The Westbrooks built a home near Ponca City, Oklahoma. Their children had children and so on. My father married my mother, Grace Jackson. Then my father decided to come to California,'' she said.

''To Tracy.''

She nodded. "And we're still here."

"The Dewberry story's not too different. I wouldn't be surprised if half the Black folks in Oklahoma came from Mississippi," he said.

"And ended up in California. Still, it's very disturbing, some of this reading. All these details. Like opening fresh wounds."

"Well, what did this last book teach you that you didn't already know?" he asked.

"I'm not sure . . ." she hesitated.

"And it disturbed you," he said.

"Maybe that's too mild. Angered would be more like it. Every time I read about those slaves packed and smothered on a slave ship, squashed together spoon-fashion, dying of disease, thirst, rat bite, and not enough air, it made me want to hurt somebody."

"Then you'd be no better than the rest of the folks. Some didn't make it, but you know that. They jumped overboard first chance they got," he said.

"And some did. Else we wouldn't be standing here," she paused, thinking.

Finally she said, "You know something, Wade, with grand ancestors like those, who came through the water watching ten million thrown overboard and survived the ship crossings from Africa, anyway, who knew about Mississippi lynchings, and lived on in spite of them . . . Sometimes fought back, who rioted, who paid for the right to live. When I think about those folks, I think about staying around here awhile. In fact, I think about living every moment of my life to its fullest until I die. Out of respect."

"Out of respect?" he repeated warmly. They embraced. Gently he massaged her earlobes. And she gave him back a sweet, lingering kiss.

"How about dinner at my house?" he offered.

She accepted.

Mississippi gumbo.

The whole table was quiet as they ate. They paid the highest tribute possible to the cook: rapt attention to the crab, shrimp, corn, chicken, hot sausage, and okra gumbo. Not a word passed a lip. Only food.

After Amber went home Wade heard the flute. For the first time in a long while she was playing again.

Later in the week, as he sat next to her on the yellow bus bumping along the country roads toward home, he read the names of the handful of books in her arms: *Touch the Earth: A Self-Portrait of Indian Existence; The Navajos; Cry of the Thunderbird; Indians of the United States; Paint the Wind.*

"Hey, Amber," he said as they parted in the middle of Clover Road, "I'll be in wrestling practice for the rest of the week after school and won't be riding the bus."

She frowned, disappointed. "A whole week? That'll be like a century."

They kissed good-bye.

"All right, then. See you later, Wade."

In her room she read and read, but each book she finished sent her deeper into a labyrinth of curiosity and wonder, and she read long into the wee hours of the morning, propped up in her bed on pillows.

"Amber, it's one A.M. Turn off the light. Go to sleep, dear," said Grace.

If she turned off the light, she did not always go to sleep. She had a flashlight under the quilt and stole a few more minutes.

Now and then she looked up from the page to see the imaginary shadows of Indians through her window. One night when she threw the covers back, she saw stars fall from the dark sky like ashes from the fireplace of God.

There was no one to go to after she finished the

books on the Indians. She didn't know any Indians. This bothered her. At least with Dr. Goldberg she got some answers. And with Susie, even though there wasn't much conversation, there was Susie's *presence*. But she didn't know any Indians, and the effect of horror after horror in all the books she had read so far weighed her down, so she withdrew a little into herself.

Early that Saturday morning she played her flute. However, it was a new sound. A warrior wail lifted from the delicate flute and invaded the day.

She was into the pain of all the experiences she had read about.

She did not go to fetch Wade and round up the boys as was her habit on Saturdays so they could get an early start on hunting and swimming.

She avoided family and friends.

At the breakfast table Johnny asked, "When's the last time you talked to Wadell? Aren't you going swimming with him this morning?"

"No," said Amber, using as few words as she could between bites of hot oatmeal.

"Some folks just don't want to be bothered," said Jason.

"Nothing but reading and music and being alone. Not even swimming and hunting with us," complained Johnny.

Amber shrugged.

She excused herself from the table early. Johnny's bushy eyebrows shot up, and a devilish grin lit up his face. "Maybe Wadell ought to personally ask her to go swimming. Who knows what goes on in the water? They say blood is thicker than water but maybe not in this case."

"I believe the young man prefers to be called Wade," said Grace.

"Have you been spying on them when they go swimming alone together?" Jason asked Johnny.

" 'Course not. But I bet you this much, she won't be slamming doors in Wadell's . . . Wade's face."

"Would you slam the door in a champion wrestler's face? Our sister might be queer, but she's not crazy."

"Who knows what Amber'll do, she doesn't belong to this family; she doesn't fit."

"I don't want to hear that again," said David. The ice in his voice shut them up.

"I was just kidding," said Jason. Then he shrugged. "But then again, it wouldn't bother me to leave her be. I've collared drumsticks three times the last three times we've had chicken, she's so preoccupied. I need that chicken, I'm growing muscles for the football team. When I get to high school, I intend to be a star fullback!"

Later on Wade appeared.

"How's Amber, Mrs. Westbrook?"

Grace grimaced. "Sometimes I have trouble understanding her, she's so different."

The melody from the flute drifted out of Amber's room and interrupted Grace's next thought.

"Least she's keeping the music up," said Wade.

"Something new."

He nodded.

Before, the songs had been recognizable ballads and old favorites, but now the sounds were different. Melancholy.

"Mrs. Westbrook, could you tell her I'm here?"

After a long while Amber came out. Her eyes set deep in her head. Her hair in one kinky finished braid down her back, as though she had been thinking and reading and braiding at the same time.

Grace left them alone.

"Amber," he said softly. "How're you doing?"

"Fine. Been busy. Reading. Music," she said.

"What are you reading?"

"Books," she said.

"Oh. Books. Thought we'd agreed to discuss the books. Have I done something wrong? I haven't seen you for a week, but you knew that. I told you beforehand . . ."

There was an awkward distance separating them. She shook her head. "It's just that . . . I mean, don't you ever feel frustrated . . . ? I mean, all this evil, they did experiments on the Jewish women in the concentration camps. And right here in America they operated on one Black woman thirty times trying to perfect their surgical skills. And now these latest books . . ."

"Discovering something you didn't know before? Is that what's bothering you?"

"I just need more time to think. I mean, who can we talk to about the Indians? I don't know any. You don't."

"That's right," he said thoughtfully.

Then he said, "Don't you want to take your mind off things a little bit? Why not let's go for a swim?"

"Can't."

"How about a walk, then?"

"I already have."

It was true. He had seen her leaving early in the morning, her backpack strapped in place, a lone figure walking toward the river. He frowned. He didn't like being left out of her thoughts.

"Why are you doing this to me?" he asked.

"What?"

"Shutting me out."

"I just—"

He touched her gently squeezing her shoulders.

She leaned against his chest. He was such a comfort.

"I just want to think about it more, that's all. Maybe it's the accumulation of all these horrors and not being able to talk to one Indian. It's got to me."

He understood and yet he didn't. He hugged her tighter, finally let her go, and went home.

Outside, before he could walk even three steps, he heard the flute.

What about Papa Westbrook?

He walked around to Amber's backyard where he saw Grandpa Westbrook stooped over, staring at the avocado tree.

"Who insulted this plant?" the older man grumbled.

Something was wrong with the avocado tree that once grew tall in the garden. Now it turned its leaves toward the ground and would not bear fruit.

He stood up from his inspection of the trunk and shook his gray head sadly.

Wade asked, "Insult a plant?"

"Oh, there are all kinds of ways. Remember the apple tree in the Matthews' old backyard?"

"The one that wouldn't give any apples after they moved away?"

"Remember how the leaves looked?"

"Looked the same to me," Wade answered, perplexed.

"But you didn't get up close and examine the veins. Now there's where you're apt to find the root of the thing."

"Sir?" asked Wade.

"Clogged veins. Shriveling and spotting the leaves."

"But how did the plant get insulted?" asked Wade.

"Don't you remember?"

"No, sir, I don't."

''The new owners tried to chop it down, then changed their minds.''

''I see.''

''Major insult,'' insisted Grandpa Westbrook.

''Didn't know plants were so sensitive.''

''Just like any living thing. They like good care.'' One hand thoughtfully brushed at his gray hair. He continued, ''Now, if a plant suffers from an insult, how much then do people suffer from meanness? Wars, genocide, and killing are catastrophic insults.''

''Plants and people,'' said Wade, thinking that in a way Amber was insulted by humanity's wrongs not made right.

''Uh-huh,'' said Papa Westbrook. ''Sensitive.''

FOUR

The twins talked between gulps of hot apple cobbler.

"What's she got in that room she's got to keep the door shut all the time?" said Jason, nodding to Amber's empty chair.

"Maybe gold," said Johnny.

"Diamonds?"

"Secret treasures of some kind."

"Something special, that's for sure."

"Under her bed she's got ten talking birds and seven witless cats."

"No, she's got a witch's broom and water for warlocks."

"Oh, it's a mess, that's for sure."

"Have you seen it, Mama?"

"What?"

"Amber's room."

"Well . . . yes."

"How do you like the way she keeps it?"

"It may not be the neatest place in the world," said Grace, exasperated with the chaos of Amber's room. "In a way, maybe it's no concern of mine. I'm not the one who's got to look at it. She does. And if it's a mess, it's her loss."

The boys exchanged glances.

"She's locked up in there again, saying she's not hungry."

Grace Westbrook compressed her lips. Her face rounded and dimpled, as though God had sunk his thumbs in the soft brown cheeks as he held her face between His hands, admiring His creation.

David Westbrook raised his eyebrows and looked thoughtfully at Amber's empty chair, then added in his rumbling voice, "She'll come out when she's good and ready."

"Don't know which I prefer, her tomboy ways or her quiet ones," Grace said.

"We did ask her to go swimming and hunting tomorrow. She said no," said Jason, scooping up another serving of apple cobbler.

"Third Saturday in a row," said Johnny.

"Ask her again. Keep asking," said Papa Westbrook, stroking his gray beard. "When my Bonnie was a young woman, she used to think a lot about things. Serious. But you couldn't find a greater sport anywhere. When she felt like hunting, horseback riding, she could beat the best of us. Only woman I ever saw defy an Oklahoma tornado. Some new adventure will bring Amber out. Just wait. Acts just like my Bonnie. She may not look like her, but she's got her spirit. Now, there was a woman even the tornado wouldn't mess with. By the way, anybody notice how funny the air is lately?"

"What do you mean, Papa?" asked David.

"Earthquake weather," said Papa.

"How do you know that?" asked Johnny.

"Yeah, how do you know?" echoed Jason. "You've only been in one minor earthquake since you moved to California. Barely registered on the Richter scale."

"I memorized the signs," said Papa.

"Papa," said David, "even the weathermen haven't learned how to forecast an earthquake the way they can predict a hailstorm or a blizzard or even a tornado. How come you can?"

"It's in the bones," he answered.

"These tremors don't usually hurt anybody," David said.

"Usually," agreed Papa. "But what happens when 'unusually' is the case?"

David nodded. "You've got a point, all right. Can't measure the damage of an earthquake until it's over. One customer thought he'd gotten away clean after that one a while back, but it had twisted his water pipes up, down where he couldn't see it. Looked all right on the surface."

"Still making road repairs from the last big one two years ago. That stretch about a quarter mile down Larch Road when you turn off Bear River," Grace said.

"Another big quake or two could split Tracy and the entire San Joaquin Valley in half," David admitted.

"As I told Amber a few weeks ago, I'm ready to go meet my Maker whenever the last trumpet sounds. My bags are always packed. And when it comes to this earthquake business, it's just a matter of time."

"Oh, Papa, what do you mean 'ready to meet your Maker'? You're not going anywhere yet," David said.

Papa answered with a dry cackle. "You've raised a good point, son. I'm kicking but not high, flopping but can't fly. But I'm still here."

Papa went back to sipping his coffee while staring longingly at Amber's chair. He missed sharing talks with his only granddaughter, who always listened to him so acutely and with the same careful attention she offered a seashell pressed to her ear or in the same way she bowed her head over her flute.

"Amber," he said to himself.

"I wonder," said Jason.

The next morning when Amber went on one of her solitary walks, the boys opened her bedroom door.

"Whew!" said Johnny. "Look a here!"

"Books. Talking about books!"

There were books everywhere. A quilt of books on the bed. Books spilling from the chest of drawers and dresser. And books carpeting the floor. They picked up a few volumes and glanced at the titles. There were books about African-Americans, Mexicans, and Asians. Books about the Holocaust. American-Indian books.

"Got more books than the city library and Tracy High combined," Johnny exaggerated with a whistle.

"Let's get out of here," Jason said, heading for the door and opening it in a rush. "Making me dizzy just staring at all these words."

"Quick. Shut the door. I think I hear her coming!" said Johnny just before they dashed down the hall.

FIVE

Just as her grandfather had predicted, Amber was coming out of her phase of study and silence.

"It's a dirty shame," she said, thinking about the Indians.

She grasped thick branches as she climbed high in the chinaberry tree growing outside the front door.

She looked down Corral Hollow Road to see if Wade and her two brothers were coming, but all she could see was the deserted road stretching to an end and the tall mountains of redwood trees far away.

Now she could hardly wait to go hunting and fishing. The twins and Wade had gone to the store to buy cartridge shells. She had promised she would meet them here by the chinaberry after they returned from shopping.

Suddenly she leaned so far forward in the treetop that her foot slipped and she almost fell. Getting a secure hold on a sturdy limb, she shook her head and blinked. She saw trees dancing. Mountains shaking like Jell-O.

The country air swelled, and the rolling distortion moved closer, disturbing everything in sight.

The chinaberry tree absorbed a shock deep in its root, a shock that spread from root to trunk, to limb, to leaf.

She stared at the house. The plate-glass window was

quickly turning yellow. Yellow berries from the chinaberry leaves rained in little thumps against the pane.

"Earthquake!" she yelled, sliding down from her perch.

Any moment the house would come crashing apart, swaying windows and all.

The vibrations continued as her boots hit the ground, then suddenly the quaking stopped, but the air smelled of sulfur, heavy and charged with danger.

She sucked in her breath and waited, dark wide eyes raking the sky, a sky of gray glass.

Then the ground groaned again beneath her feet. She hugged the drunken tree while the gray-glass sky turned to gray-slate.

On the other side of the yard, bushes of bunchberry and devil's paintbrush trembled and reeled.

Dazed, she leaned her head against the rough bark of the tree while dizziness swooped over her.

The spasm went on.

From every side she heard the jolting rumble that troubled the tree and sent the glass pane shimmying again.

"Amber!" her mother called from the house. "where are you?"

But Amber was too preoccupied to answer. She was busy digging her boots into the soil, her head cocked to one side, listening.

The unbroken roar of the earthquake knocked shingles off the house. Loosened the red bricks on the chimney until they rained from the roof.

Kerplunk.

She ducked down by the chinaberry to keep from getting hit.

Kerplunk.

Next the earthquake cut a wide swath clear across Clover Road, splitting the asphalt.

"Whoa!" Amber shouted.

But the earthquake spoke again, and as it spoke, the earth rumbled with worry.

"Amber Marie Westbrook!" Grace screamed.

But Amber was concentrating her attention on the earthquake that California legend called the avenging angel of the Indians, a red angel who stepped out of the river now and then to make his presence known.

Kerplunk.

"Go back to the river where you belong," Amber said.

The ground shifted again, ready to gape open and swallow her.

The thought of being gobbled up by the earth paralyzed her, and she could not move even if she wanted to.

"Go back to water," she whispered.

The earthquake, who perhaps wanted to be listened to, finally heard her. And soon, through a great act of will, the earthquake ceased to tremble, wrapped himself in his shawl of turquoise and jade, and started back to the waves of the river.

Before the earthquake could reach the river home, Amber had scrambled into her own home and into the arms of Grace.

"Now, that was more than a tremble," said Grace, hugging Amber to her. "Wonder if your daddy and the boys are all right."

"And Wade," Amber said, her eyes wide as she surveyed the awesome damage. "And Grandpa?"

"He slept right through it. Nothing disturbs his afternoon nap."

The phone rang.

"Probably Daddy checking in now."

"Your daddy's fine," Grace said as she hung up the phone. "Now, I wonder where the boys are?"

"Let's go outside and look," Amber suggested.

Amber put her hand over her brow and looked off down the road. "Here they come, Mama."

"Well, that's a relief," Grace said.

They looked around.

"Looks like we lost part of the chimney, and Corral Hollow Road's messed up," said Amber.

Grace leaned over and picked up a damaged shingle, while Amber gathered the chimney bricks and piled them near the porch.

Next they walked over to the road and inspected the split the road crew would have to repair.

Spiders and long earthworms crawled out of the earth's interior.

"So glad we're all safe," said Grace, watching the boys' approach.

Amber followed her gaze. "Finally we're going swimming and hunting. At last," said Amber, as though somebody else besides herself had kept her from the river and the woods.

Grace thought a moment. She was glad Amber was interested in being with her brothers and Wade again, but the fear of the earthquake made her cautious. "Come on in the house. Another quake might come, and you don't have sense enough to come in out of the rain, even when it's raining bricks!"

"Well, what about later today?"

"Not today. And when they get here, I'll tell them I said to stay put too."

"Wade can't go with us tomorrow. Tomorrow he's got wrestling practice."

"On Sunday?"

"Well, when you're the champ, you have to work when the challengers are sleeping. At least that's what Wade always claims."

"I said no."

She recognized that final note in her mother's voice. Nothing would budge her. Amber stood looking at the mess the earthquake had made, wondering if it had been satisfied by the time it made it on back to its home where the river dipped into the sea.

She shrugged. She looked over at Grace. Her mother looked like the light was hurting her eyes. Amber knew if she spoke another word of protest, Grace's head would start to ache. Now and then her mother got headaches, migraines, real bad.

Better to go to Bear River tomorrow.

She stepped over the rift in the road and went inside the house.

No is my mother's favorite word, she decided.

SIX

A flood of rose petals, upset by the earthquake, lay stunned on the lawn. The air, which was charged before, seemed to settle itself so the roses could breathe.

Somehow the settled day reminded Amber of her mother. A prim day. A woman's day, a frilly day. An inside-the-house day.

Because of the earthquake Amber was confined to the house. The closest she could get to outside was to stare out the window.

When she was younger, on rainy days she now and then disappeared up to the attic. How long had it been? Years since she had ventured into that musky place, out of the range of her mother's neat glare.

Now, although the attic belonged to the house, it was not like her mother. It was not like the rest of the house. It was more like her room. An outcast in a neat home. The attic was disheveled. In a jumble. Disordered, like the out-of-doors in a way. A wilderness.

One by one she climbed the stairs, puffs of dust flying up around her feet. Nobody had been up here in ages, certainly not her mama with her relentless dust mop, she thought, sneezing as she pushed opened the attic door to enter the small room.

Just a little light filtered through the slatted small window, not enough to see much by and hardly any fresh air at all. She pulled the chain on the attic light;

nothing happened. "Bulb's out," she whispered to herself the way people often do in the dark.

Although it was dark, the place was still a mine field. "A-choo!" she sneezed again, hurrying her way to the small arrow of light in the wall.

But before she could reach it, she tripped over an abandoned doll and tumbled. She got up and dusted herself off. Now she more carefully inched toward the window.

If she pushed hard enough on the small slatted window, it would open just a wedge. "There," she said, breathing in the fresh flow of air. The breath of flowers didn't reach this high up, but at least the air diluted the dust.

In the middle of the collected clutter a fringe shawl covered a thick trunk. Here she sat in the semilight, her chin in her hand, elbow on her knee.

Where to start?

She looked around. Old paintings, old hats hung on nails; one of a set of high-heeled shoes, looking orphaned away from its mate, pointed a golden pinched toe at her; an ancient table whose surface she once crayoned pictures on sat patiently in the corner; her first baby bed looking ready for occupancy, reminded her that time moves on and that she was fifteen now. All of these wonders lived in the attic.

The place comforted her. In the attic nobody had cared if she left her crayons out, or if the high-heeled shoes she hiked around in while wearing her mother's old-fashioned skirts were left out of their boxes.

In the old days, when she was tired of playing here, she had always sat and daydreamed on this very trunk. She had called it her throne.

The trunk. Why not start here? She had taken the trunk for granted. It had been her special seat. And she had thought of it only as a place to sit. Not a trunk.

"Why, I could be sitting on top of a treasure!"

She slid off the trunk and knelt before it. She pulled the shawl away. "Padlocked!"

It was the first time she had ever seen anything under lock and key in this house.

"Why?" she wondered out loud.

She pulled a hairpin out of her braid and started working at the lock.

Her fingers trembled with curiosity and frustration, and she dropped the pin more than once.

But she was persistent.

On and on she turned the pin, this way and that.

By the time the lid's lock, rusty and old, gave way, her braid had undone itself and stood out like a kinky halo around her head.

"What have we here?" she said, peering in. "A bundle of old scrapbooks!"

She opened the one on top, a brown, fragile looseleaf binder. On the first page she saw her daddy dressed in an air force uniform, his head held high and proud.

She paused a moment, considering him. No wonder Mama married him. He's so handsome. The bald spot had not claimed the top of his head yet. She turned to the facing page. Across from that photo she discovered a picture of her mother in a frilly evening gown, in the standard pose for a high school prom, a carnation pinned on her bosom, a flirting twinkle in her eyes. Why, she looks like she never had a migraine in her life, Amber thought.

She kept rummaging until she came to the scrapbook at the very bottom of the box. More pictures. "Now, wherever in the world did Mama find a ribbon that large?" she wondered out loud, studying the school photo of herself taken at the kindergarten door. Somebody had written on the back: "Amber's first official day of education.'' The writing seemed to be that of her mother's neatly controlled hand.

Her father's scrawl turned up every now and then, especially on the backs of her twin brothers' snapshots. There Johnny and Jason were, babies, looking like two black-eyed peas in a pod, one's arm over the other, sound asleep in an oversize blue bassinet. But which one was which?

Even back then they looked mischievous. As if saying, ''Guess who?''

When had their mischief begun?

She couldn't remember. They'd always been a bother as much as she loved them. Even before they were born they had been a bother, acting up as they did in the middle of her Easter poem. Easter service, her first public appearance at three years old, and what did they do? Sent her mother into labor. The boys were on their way. She never did finish that poem. She had gone with her parents, refusing to stay with the other church members who offered to baby-sit for her. She had to see. They had to rush from Sunday School to the hospital, the rest of the Easter poem still turning in her head. She was sitting with her father in a hospital waiting room instead of thrashing bushes for Easter eggs. At last Dr. Goldberg announced that the twins were born. Hand in hand with her father, they hurried to the hospital's plate-glass window, and what did she see?

Two boys. Their bald heads looking like two Easter eggs.

She turned the page. A picture of her in a christening dress.

''My lands, I look so serious.''

Wonder when this was taken? The picture was so fragile, the edges peeled into her hand. Is there a date behind it?

She was afraid to handle the photo too much, afraid it might crumble all to shreds in her hand.

Maybe she'd better leave well enough alone.

She started to turn the page. Carefully—but her thumb brushed the picture.

There was something under the photo. Like padding.

She fingered the thick surface.

Probably nothing. Maybe another picture, her at one day old, right after she was born?

Her curiosity leapt, catlike, to the top of her head, then sprang down to her searching fingers.

The christening picture came out easily enough. She quickly turned it over to find a date scribbled in bold blue printing on the back.

She looked down at what was left on the page, expecting to see the baby picture.

"Well, it's definitely not a picture," she said.

Left on the scrapbook page was a folded piece of paper. Yellow with age.

She unraveled it.

The ink was faint, smeared with water drops or teardrops. She screwed up her eyes, trying to decipher the lines.

After a moment she could make out the first word, but she needed more light.

She walked over to the little shuttered window, where the light flowed steadier and stronger. Now there was light enough, all right.

It was a letter. Dated back before she was even born. Ancient.

Probably a love letter between her mother and her father.

Thinking of the handsome young man and the pretty young woman of the photographs, this possibility of passion notes between her parents fascinated her. She leaned over closer to the window light. Now she could see better.

"Dear Aunt Grace and Uncle David . . ."

No, it was not *between* her mother and father, it was *to* them.

She read on.

Her eyes skipped to the bottom of the page.

Oh, it's from cousin Abyssinia when she was in med school, a thank-you note for their wedding gift.

Then it was not a secret love letter from her father to her mother or vice versa. She yawned and started to fold the letter back up, but out of the bottom of her eye she thought she saw the word *pregnant.*

Pregnant?

She quickly spread the paper out again and leaned toward the light.

"We are pregnant, expecting a child (a girl, we think) around the last of February or the first of March. . . . We wonder if you might be interested in taking this baby?"

The first of March . . . A girl? *But that's when I was born. . . .*

As the impact of her discovery slammed into her mind, she crushed the yellow paper in her trembling hand.

"Maybe my eyes were playing tricks on me," she whispered, and she spread the paper out again. She studied it over and over. "Oh, it's true. It's true! They lied to me!"

There was a place in her, on the left of her brain, where rage and pain lived. It was the place most affected when she witnessed oppression, when she read about the ill treatment of anybody. Now that place in her mind quaked with anger.

"They threw me away! Like an old hand-me-down dress!"

She could not deny the evidence of her own ill treatment. And it was not found in one of her books or in *Ebony* magazine but in this single sheet of paper kept hidden in this dark attic.

As she studied the yellow paper the rage and pain distilled into a tiny drop of liquid. Then the single jeweled tear slid down her face and silenced her moving lips.

And then, as if by reflex, as though she had a hold on something hot, some yellow flame, a burning insult, that echoed the outrage of every persecuted group and slammed her head with a pain reminding her of the one she felt for the Blacks, the Jews, the Japanese, the Indians, her grip loosened, her hand opened swiftly, and the paper fluttered to the floor.

Her mind could not easily deal with the discovery. She focused on a golden narrow-toed shoe, everything else in her vision's periphery blurred. She was crushed. A compacted chest. No breath. A half-hypnotized invalid. What was that sound? It was coming from way up high. You can't get any higher in this house than this. Is it raining? Why, it never rains in the summer. When she peeked through the attic slats, it was only raining sunbeams. Yet on the ground, where the sunbeams splashed, the red petals of June roses had fallen like red petals of rain.

SEVEN

Amber, Jason and Johnny coming out of their driveway were dressed and set for the Saturday hunt and swim.

They waved across the road to Wade, who hailed them from his open screen door.

He wished he could join them. He wanted to talk to Amber. She hadn't spoken much since yesterday, the day of the earthquake. And last night she had been shut up in her room. He sighed. Given the last few weeks, her silence was not all that unusual. But yesterday when they were getting ready to go hunting, he thought she had come out of her stupor.

"Well, at least she's getting out again," he said to himself with relief, then he yelled out loud, "Amber, catch something for me, a rabbit big enough to make the stew kettle smell. Remember what I told you, Johnny, a wrestler needs good nourishment. Right, Jason?"

"Have a good practice," the boys called.

Amber, her aqua swimsuit tucked in the back pocket of her jeans, adjusted the shotgun across her shoulders. Then she balanced the huge pack on her back.

When she and the boys got farther down the road, she turned around to wave to Wade, but he had already disappeared back into his house, preparing to get to wrestling practice on time. She waved to Grace and Papa, who were still standing on the porch.

"Leading the way again," said Grace. They thought

she looked more like her old self once more, with Jason and Johnny bringing up the rear.

"What you got in that backpack, Amber?" one of the twins goodnaturedly asked as they hiked down Corral Hollow Road. "A couch?"

"No more than I need," said Amber. She felt as though she were carrying a mountain of pain on her back. She didn't feel very much like joking with anybody today.

Grace, at her station on the porch, squinched up her eyes. It seemed that Amber's backpack looked larger than usual.

"Eyes are acting funny," she said, shaking her head.

"What?"

"Nothing, Papa." Then, "I had to bite my tongue to keep from telling Amber to stay. I'd trust the boys more in an earthquake than I would Amber. Sometimes she just doesn't show good sense, something to do with that curiosity of hers. . . ."

"At least she's up and out, away from her room and those books. Be thankful for small blessings," Papa said as he turned to go tend the garden. "I can't believe I napped right through it."

"As you say," Grace repeated, "be thankful for small blessings."

Before long, after passing through the evergreen forest and a variety of redwoods, Amber and the twins came upon Bear River.

It took Amber only half a minute behind the sweet gum-tree to step into her swimsuit.

"Get ready. Get set. Go."

All three dived into the water at once. A great splashing filled the air as arms and legs flew through the water.

"Told you she learned to swim before she could walk," said Jason as Amber beat them to the other side.

"Didn't I tell you she's not our sister? They found her in a pond," said Johnny, floating on his back.

"What's the matter, Amber, lost your sense of humor?" said Jason at the stricken look on her face.

The look gave way to a half smile.

They dog-paddled, did the butterfly stroke, the breaststroke, splashing and kicking until their fingers and toes were waterlogged.

After a while they stopped swimming.

It was a bright day for hunting, and the air smelled of river and pine.

As they began the hunting phase of their Saturday outing, as usual, Amber led the way, her shotgun ready. Her piercing eyes spied the rabbit first. And their guns went up.

As the shot rang out she remembered a shudder in Grace's eyes and had visions of the rabbit up against the wall, herself the chief executioner.

After the rabbit was downed she knelt over him. But there was none of the old jubilation. The surging sense of triumph followed by proud laughter was missing.

For a moment her brothers thought she was praying, she was so still over the dead bunny.

"Here, take him on home," she said, handing the rabbit to Johnny and looking away. "Think I'll pick some wildflowers. Thought I saw some jewelweeds over there."

"All right," said Jason, looking taller and skinnier than she remembered. Johnny, beside him, looked like his mirror image. In unison they turned away from her in the direction of home.

Soon her brothers were in step, walking briskly down Bear River Road.

For a long time she stood watching them move down the road until she could not see them anymore.

Then she turned and started walking in the other direction, her backpack secure.

EIGHT

Back at the house on Corral Hollow Road, Grace lay napping. Breathing softly, she dreamed of her children. One of them, with back turned, was fading from sight.

Suddenly she sat straight up in bed, strict as stone. A foreign wind whispered through the screen and shivered along the nape of her neck.

In the distance a car rumbled down Corral Hollow Road like a prehistoric monster clearing its throat.

Her frayed voice erupted, "Jason!" and she thought she heard a dark burst of thunder, but the sky was still. "Johnny! Amber!"

Now she pulled the white cotton sheet off and sprang to the floor.

She ran through the archway separating the bedroom from the living room and stopped as though a force had broken her flight just in front of the screen door.

The sound of running feet coming down the road from the direction of the river filled all the jagged corners of the house.

Danger hitched a ride on the hurried feet of the runner.

She shaded her eyes and looked down the road. Instead of three children she saw only two.

A channel of air whisked in from the screen door, but it did not cool her. A gust of weeping heat.

She carefully glued her eyes on the advancing figures.

She recognized the approaching gingham shirt. The particular gait. The careful sling of the gun over the shoulders. She could make out who it was running down the road from the river now. It was Jason.

One hand fluttered over her heart, and the other hand hesitantly touched the screen door handle.

"Jason, what happened?" Then, before he could answer, she asked, "Where's Johnny? Where's Amber?"

"They're coming. Nothing . . . nothing happened."

Did she see glinting shadows in her son's eyes?

Something she could not put into words hung in the air. She glanced nervously down the road at her other son trudging along, the rabbit in one hand.

"Johnny?" Grace said when he reached the house, "is everything all right?"

"Sure, Mama," he answered.

"Where's Amber?" Grace asked as the twins hung their guns over the fireplace.

"Oh, she'll be along."

"You know I don't like her left alone. You know that." Sighing because she thought she was again falling into that everlasting habit of being overanxious about her children, she said, "I think I'd better lie back down. I had the most disturbing dream."

"What was it?" Jason asked.

"I thought . . ." she began, then stopped, throwing up her hands. "Just a stupid dream." She walked back into her bedroom shaking her head.

About an hour later David Westbrook pulled up in the driveway.

Grace got up and put on a pot of coffee as Papa came in from gardening. She sat out a can of condensed Carnation milk, and a little porcelain glass jar of sugar.

''How was your day?'' she asked.

''Okay, except I had to repair that Taylor woman's toilet again.''

''Again? What's this, the tenth time?''

''Uh-huh. You know, the tenants never were home when I went there before. Today they were. Now I understand.''

''What?''

''When a three-hundred-pound woman sits down on a toilet stool, it's been used. Where's Amber?'' he asked.

''Must be at Wade's,'' Jason said.

''Time for her to come home,'' David said. Grace dialed across the road. ''Hello, this is Grace. Would you tell Amber it's time to come home for dinner? . . . Oh. . . . Thank you. Good-bye.''

She hung up the phone, puzzled. ''Now, where could that child be? Too late for her to be out.''

''Somewhere quenching that colored curiosity, no doubt,'' Johnny said.

''Where could she ever be?'' said Grace.

''She'll be here by the time the table's set,'' David said.

''I do wish she wasn't so adventuresome,'' Grace complained.

''No such thing,'' David said.

Papa Westbrook nodded his head in agreement.

''Well, she does go too far sometimes. Remember the Priscilla Redwine incident?'' Grace said.

''Priscilla Redwine? How could anybody forget Amber and the Priscilla Redwine episode?'' Jason and Johnny chimed.

''Who was Priscilla Redwine?'' asked Papa.

''Let me tell it,'' said Johnny.

''No, I will,'' Jason said.

NINE

A couple of years ago Grace Westbrook and Mrs. Dewberry, Wade's mother, had been discussing Priscilla Redwine, the woman everybody claimed couldn't have children.

"Why can't she have babies?" Amber had asked.

"They took all her equipment away," Grace said.

"What?" asked Amber.

"Womb. Ovaries. Both breasts. Where would she put a child? What would she nourish it with?"

"Cow's milk?" Amber asked.

"She might. Me, I don't believe in heifers nursing children," Wade's mother had said.

"I thought a heifer was a cow who never had a calf."

"In this case I mean a cow that never gave birth to a human."

"Oh."

"Babies who drink cow's milk are always up in some doctor's office. And the hospital stays full of bottle babies."

"So where'd she find this baby she keeps wheeling up and down Corral Hollow Road in that carriage?" Grace had asked.

"Nobody knows. Best little child in the world, though. Never once heard her cry. Not a peep," Mrs. Dewberry said.

''So it's a girl, then?''

''Judging from the pink frills and ribbons on the carriage, it's got to be.''

''Ever see the face?'' Amber wondered out loud.

''Never.''

''Think some unfortunate young girl had it and left it on Priscilla's doorstep?'' Mrs. Dewberry asked.

''Must,'' said Grace.

Other Tracy people were not as kind as Amber's and Wade's mothers.

Amber had heard snatches of enough mean conversations from the gossipy females to verify this lack of kindness.

''Who would have Priscilla Redwine even if she did have all her organs?'' one woman asked.

''Night gets dark,'' the other one replied.

''You act like a man loses his memory when the sun goes down. I don't care how dark it gets, how's he gonna forget a face like that?''

''Well, honey, you're not married, either.''

''I'm biding my time. Waiting for Mr. Right. Know I'll get me a man before she ever will. Face all wrinkled like chitlings. Talking about ugly! Why, my feet look better than her face.''

For some time the country folk had been wondering about Priscilla Redwine. Always talk, talk, talk behind her back.

Still, every day the sun was out, Amber could see Priscilla pushing that baby carriage. Whenever anybody approached, she would cover the child up.

''Don't come near us with your bacterias,'' she would fuss the minute adults looked like they were about to get too close to the buggy. ''Get your old folks' germs on from around this innocent child's breath!''

And then Amber would see Priscilla running for

home, pushing the carriage and flying down the road as if ten demons were after her. She would run in her front door and close it. People could hear the locks clicking. Then, after peering out the windows, she would draw the curtains shut. And that was that.

Two hobos walking down the road figured it out.

"I doubt if anybody's in that buggy, anyway. Mighty strange we never hear the baby cry. All babies cry, that's a universal fact."

"Something dirty's in the milk all right," the other hobo said, after thinking carefully about the situation and readjusting his bedroll on his back. "Ain't nothing in that carriage but air and blankets."

"Anyway, everybody knows Priscilla Redwine is a little touched in the head. Crazy as a California earthquake. Her daddy was an undertaker. Living 'round dead folks'll drive anybody nuts."

"Wasn't only dead folk. Dead elk. Dead eagles. And dead owls. Redwine, best taxidermist in the county."

It was true that after Mr. Redwine the mortician died, Priscilla closed the doors and turned the laying-out room into a living room. People had to take their dead elsewhere. They could no longer walk past the mortuary window where they used to inspect the dead lying out in their caskets, dressed up for viewing with stuffed deer, hawks, and bears' heads staring down at them from the walls. Now Priscilla stood in her window for herself where she could look out toward the sequoia-covered hills and mountains as she rocked the baby in her arms.

Well, a few months went by, and still nobody had seen Priscilla Redwine's infant.

Then Amber thought, Wouldn't it be wonderful if she was the first person in the countryside to see Priscilla Redwine's baby? Now, that would be quite an accomplishment.

The minute she thought it, she had already begun to prepare to do it. She wanted to tell Wade, but the thrill of keeping it a secret and a surprise changed her mind.

In order to accomplish the feat she had to study Priscilla's habits.

Amber noticed that whenever Priscilla came outside, she always had the baby with her. You see Priscilla, you see the carriage pushed in front of her.

Every day, just about, Priscilla went to the store and bought fresh vegetables, a carton of milk, and a jar of baby food. She also never failed to buy her favorite chocolate-chip cookies.

The baby was eating well; the grocer had told everyone. But he had not seen the baby's face, either, although the pair frequented the store daily. The baby's little head and entire body were covered up as a protection against pneumonia, flu, and TB.

"Funny how that baby never protests all those blankets weighing down on her head," said the grocer, lacing his hands over his fishbowl belly. "Always sleeping. Guess Priscilla waits till it's nap time to do her shopping so she's not disturbed by all that hollering."

"Maybe she feeds it some of her chocolate-chip cookies," somebody said.

And that's when Amber got the idea of how to get into Priscilla's house. She knew that Priscilla had a yen for chocolate-chip cookies. Amber would sell her some, hot from the oven. The last time Amber had sold the Redwines cookies was when Mr. Redwine was alive. And he always bought two dozen, claiming Priscilla would eat the entire twenty-four cookies in one sitting.

Amber smiled, thinking about how she would be the

first person in Tracy to see the child. Then she would tell Wade if the baby's cheeks were fat, if her eyes sparkled, if she smiled back at you when you tickled her chin, if she had ten fingers, ten toes, and if she looked anything at all like Priscilla Redwine.

As far as Amber could tell, the only time Priscilla was not with the baby was when she took her nightly bath. Amber discovered this after watching the house for a week.

It took Amber a week to determine that the lights went off in Priscilla Redwine's house every night at nine fifty-five precisely. Then it took her another week to discover that the bathroom windows were steamed up at about nine-thirty every night. So the best time to see the Redwine baby was between nine-thirty and nine-fifty, a twenty-minute span.

Getting inside was the difficult part.

That afternoon, after Priscilla had done all her grocery shopping and was settled in for the evening, Amber rang the door bell.

Priscilla answered the door, babe in arms almost smothered in pink blankets.

"Yes?"

"Miss Priscilla, I have some chocolate-chip cookies fresh made. Just popped them out of the oven."

Priscilla's nose had already identified the delightful aroma.

"Let me get you some money. How much?"

"Same as usual. Dollar a dozen."

"I'll take two dollars worth, then."

Which is what Amber knew she would say. Amber quickly stepped inside the house at this opportune moment. The fragrant cookies in front of her, like so much bait.

"If you're busy with the baby, I can hold her for you," Amber said, and she reached for the bundle.

Priscilla backed away, pulling the baby closer to her. "Wait. No, wait." She checked her dress pocket, jingling some change.

Oh, no, I hadn't counted on that, thought Amber, that she would have the change on her person.

Priscilla counted out one dollar.

"You just want one dozen, then?" asked Amber, holding the change.

Priscilla thought a moment, looking from the baby bundle to Amber, who wanted to hold the baby, and then to the cookie bag dangling in Amber's hand.

Then she decided, "Well, just a minute. Stand right there. I'll be right back." And she hurried away, keeping the baby on her hip.

The minute the woman was out of sight, Amber unlocked the window by the door.

When Priscilla came back into the room, her eyes seemed to stray to the window. Or did they? Amber guiltily wondered. Priscilla shifted the baby to her other hip and handed Amber a dollar bill in exchange for the cookie bag.

"Thank you, Miss Priscilla."

"You're welcome," answered Priscilla as she shut the door, clicking the double lock.

At the dinner table that evening Amber could barely contain herself.

"Why're you so fidgety?" Grace had asked.

"Oh, nothing," said Amber.

The twins turned their eyes upon her. Their noses sniffed the air, smelling danger, adventure.

"What's up, Amber?"

"Nothing."

"Why're you so excited?"

"I'm not excited."

"The few times I've ever known you to eat everything on your plate and ask for seconds is when you're excited about something. Something secret,'' said Johnny.

''Leave Amber alone,'' David had said. ''She's got a right to be reflective.''

And that was the end of their interrogation and just about the end of dinner.

After helping her brothers clean the kitchen Amber joined the family for a game of Monopoly. After she had acquired as much money and property as she could, she said good night and turned in early to read her novel until it was time.

But she could not concentrate. She could not follow the plot of the story. Her eyes kept straying from the page and to the clock on her night stand.

After a few long hours it was nine o'clock.

She tiptoed out the back door and went racing down the road until she came in sight of Priscilla Redwine's house. She slowed her pace. It was only about nine-fifteen, so she had fifteen minutes to wait. What would she do for fifteen minutes?

She stationed herself in the backyard under the loganberry bush where she had waited so many hours before to ascertain Priscilla's schedule. She had waited more patiently then, but tonight she was as impatient as ants.

And she felt guilty. Entering somebody's house without permission was serious business. Although her father never hit her, she was sure he would scalp her alive if he knew about this adventure.

But then she thought about being the first person in Tracy to see Priscilla's baby, and her guilt took a backseat.

She looked up and saw the bathroom light go on. Then it's time, she said to herself. She stealthily crept to the front door and, bending low, soon reached the window she had unlocked earlier.

She raised the window quickly, then heard a door shut somewhere inside the house. Had she come too soon? Was Priscilla Redwine just brushing her teeth and had come back to check the baby before taking her bath? Was she coming to recheck the doors and windows?

Amber held her breath.

Then she heard the bathwater running and sighed a sigh of relief.

She stepped inside the house and carefully closed the window.

Now the baby.

The house was as still as a mortuary at midnight. Not a sound could she hear. She had hoped for a cry or at least a baby giggle.

To get to the bedroom where she supposed the baby was, she had to go through the kitchen. Kitchen cabinet doors stood open, exposing row after row of baby food jars unopened.

She gave an involuntary gasp. If Priscilla was hoarding all this baby food she bought every day, what was the baby eating?

She kept walking and soon forgot about the baby food when she spied the crib in the bedroom. And in the middle of the crib rested a bundle.

She sped to the baby bed.

There was a baby in there, all right. The hobos had been wrong about that. This was much more than air and blankets. And certainly too big for a doll.

She pulled the pink, frilly blankets aside, and her eyes almost popped out of her head. She was petrified with amazement. Her tongue froze in her mouth, and her throat turned to a cavern of aching ice that would not thaw.

"Who???" she finally whispered when her throat relaxed.

"Who?

"Who?" sounding like an owl who-ing hoarsely in the evening.

She had seen stuffed bears, stuffed elk, and stuffed tigers before, but never in the entirety of her life had she ever seen a stuffed baby.

She leaned over the crib and peered closer. The baby eyes were black with lacquered lashes. The cheeks plump and dimpled. The tender arms as soft as cotton to the touch.

"Who?" said Amber.

"Who, who, *who,* WHO!" She finally screamed so loud, the whole house shook. She jerked her hands away from the crib bars so violently, she upset the entire cradle. The stuffed baby rolled on the floor and kept staring at her with her lacquered eyelashed eyes.

"Who!" Amber took off running, vaguely aware that Priscilla Redwine's bathroom door was opening.

She didn't stop to look at the woman. She didn't turn around. She ran through the kitchen with its cabinets of unopened food. She ran through the living room and reached the front entrance.

She unclicked the locks and jerked the door open, almost pulling the knob out of its socket.

She ran down Corral Hollow Road hollering, "WHO? WHO? WHO?" and on into her driveway, forgetting her stealthy plan of careful deceit to tiptoe home through the back door with none the wiser about her little secret trip. Forgetting about how in the morning she was going to smugly describe the Priscilla Redwine baby to Wade and to all who would listen with open mouths.

"WHO?"

Running. Running. Running to her own house.

Her front door swung open, and her father, mother, and twin brothers stood with their eyes stretched, taken back by the image of Amber running toward them hollering "WHO?"

Her father caught her, held her, stroked her head, and asked, "Amber, Amber, what happened? Did somebody bother you? Calm down and tell me, baby, what's wrong?"

But all Amber could say was, "WHO? WHO? WHO?"

It had been Wade who dashed across the road and who finally calmed her down so they could hear what happened. In a strange way it had happened just as she had planned, with Wade and the others listening with open mouths. But it took all of them, including Wade, keeping a steady eye on her that made even the telling of it possible.

That was another time. Now the family sat in the living room waiting for Amber and wondering where she was. Jason's retelling of the Priscilla Redwine story only reminded Grace of the fantastic lengths to which Amber would go to soothe her curiosity.

"An insatiable appetite for knowing," Grace decided.

"You must admit, though," David said, "some good came out of Amber's detective work. It did get that Priscilla Redwine some help. Social workers and doctors galore."

"For truth?" said Papa, enchanted by the episode that had taken place before his arrival. "That's my Amber, all right."

"But where is she?" Grace wondered.

"Seems to me that the Priscilla Redwine incident started with a walk too. And look how long she was gone that time," Johnny said.

"Gone for hours and we didn't even know it. Slipping out each night to time that woman," Grace said.

''But where is she?'' Grace insisted. ''Lord, I hope she didn't go on one of her unusual hunting trips.''

''We already did the hunting, Mama,'' said Johnny. ''I tell you, she was headed home. She'll be here soon.''

''She'd better,'' said Grace, a motherly threat in her voice. She was remembering with clarity that extraordinary hunting episode that day last year.

TEN

"We have a tomboy on our hands, I think," Grace said from the couch, looking up at the gun rack with its one empty place. Evening shadows dappled the shining oakwood floor and bounced against the brick fireplace. Grace was thinking of another Saturday morning when Wade was away at a wrestling match and the twins had gone with him. "A girl born with adventure in her blood.

Amber had gotten up that day last year, frisky as a pup, and declared that she was going for a walk, claiming that even the very pine trees in the distance beckoned her to come and enjoy the day.

"Go ahead," Grace had agreed reluctantly as she folded bathroom towels and other freshly dried laundry. "But don't go hunting alone. I don't like the idea of you out by yourself with a gun. What if you accidentally shot yourself?"

"I won't, Mama. Haven't you said that I am a fantastic markswoman?"

"Yes, Amber, you are. And you're careful too. It's just that sometimes your thirst for adventure frightens me. Heaven knows, I'm not sure why. You're so bold, if you met up with a bear, I declare I'd have to pray, 'Lord, please have mercy on the bear.' But then again, you don't have sense enough to be afraid of anything."

"Look, Mama, no gun," Amber said, showing her that the gun was still in its rack over the living-room fireplace.

She embraced her mother and soon had bounded out of the front door. Instead of taking Corral Hollow Road she struck out across the field. On the far horizon cows, like mobile brown shrubs against the hillside, chewed their cuds and fussed at flies with their tails.

As she ambled through pastures she watched blue jays pipe through the air, their flashing wings riding the wind. All around her life quivered: the ghostlike gum trees throbbing with the shrill dronings of cicadas and the small sounds of bugs hurrying and fat bees humming.

A jackrabbit leapt up in the field and went bounding through a maze of sage.

And then she saw the prize she would take home.

She got down on her belly and moved as quietly as an Indian in a Western movie.

Before she could say *lightning*, she had it.

Holding her treasure in one hand, she started back to her house.

There, she found Grace sitting in the living-room rocker, humming to herself. She tiptoed up from behind and covered her mother's eyes with one hand.

"Mama, I got a surprise for you. Can you guess what?"

"Will you give me some clues?"

"Yes."

"What color is it?"

"Guess."

"Blue?"

"No."

"Green?"

"No."

"Yellow?"

"Yes."

"Is that the only color?"

"No."

"Lots of colors?"

"No."

"One more color?"

"Yes."

"Purple?"

"No."

"Black?"

"Yes."

"So it's yellow and black. Inanimate?"

Amber hesitated. "Yes, it's dead."

"Yellow and black. Hmmm. Inanimate. What could it be? Is it something to eat?"

"No. You wouldn't."

"Oh. I know what it is!" Grace said, clapping her hands together. "You've brought me a flower. A lovely yellow flower with black eyes. A black-eyed Susan. Oh, Amber!" And she jumped up from the rocker and turned around with a delighted smile on her face.

But her joy quickly evaporated. In one hand Amber held a headless three-foot-long rattlesnake.

"Amber!"

"Oh, Mama, it can't hurt you."

"Put that dreadful thing down."

"But it's dead."

"Obviously, but how . . . ?"

"I killed it."

"What? How?" Grace gave Amber one long, despairing look and threw up her hands. "No, I don't want to hear about it. Amber Westbrook, you go to your room till your father gets here. And get that thing out of my sight."

"Oh, Mama."

"Go, you hear?"

"Land's sake. It's just an old dead snake."

"And you killed it. What if that viper had bitten you? And there you'd be out in the middle of nowhere dying from snakebite."

"But it didn't bite me. And I killed it."

"Lord, have mercy. What did I do to deserve this fate? A tomboy daughter with not enough sense to leave some of God's creatures be. Just wait until David gets home. You just wait." And Grace went to her room, saying, "I feel a migraine coming." She lay across her bed mumbling, "A daughter who hunts snakes . . ."

Amber had been so pleased when she first saw the snake. She had gotten down on her knees and flattened herself out, slinking along on her belly Indian-style, quiet and quick, until she came right upon the rattler.

From the back of the diamond-checkered serpent, she shot out her hands as quick as lightning and grabbed his tail. With a swift flick of her wrist, *pop*, she had whipped the snake's head off his neck.

She had gone home to show off her trophy to her brothers and Wade, hoping they were back from the wrestling match, but they were not there. Then she had seen Grace and impulsively decided to play a little mischief on her mother, but it had backfired and now she had to spend a boring afternoon in her room. Thank God for books; otherwise she would be as dead as the rattler from boredom.

She went outside and buried the snake and came back to her bedroom and picked up a book to read.

From down the hall she could hear Grace mumbling to the air, "A daughter who hunts snakes . . ."

* * *

''She's just brave, that's all,'' admitted Jason begrudgingly as he held up the wall between the living room and the dining room.

''I wish I could have seen the look on Mama's face when Amber shook that old snake at her,'' said Johnny, his long frame stretched out on the round rug so that his feet hit the hardwood floor and his head rested against the soft hooked carpet of flowers.

David, who sat next to Grace, looked a little worried but tried not to show it. ''I'm giving her a piece of my mind when she gets home this time.''

''I'd like to see her snake out of this one,'' said Jason, stretching out next to Johnny.

''Think she could be at Wade's by now?'' Johnny asked.

Just then, a familiar scratch at the door. They all jumped, but it was only Wade. ''Amber here yet?'' he asked.

''Oh, Amber, Amber,'' whispered Grace, ''where are you?''

ELEVEN

"I was hoping she'd be here by now," Wade said, "After today's practice, smelling sweating wrestlers and squeezing my opponents' rusty necks into Nelson holds, I'm ready for the sweet smell of women and something more delicate for my fingers to do. They're itching to touch the cello strings. I thought Amber might want to play a duet after dinner."

David stared stonily at his watch and drummed his thick fingers on the couch arm. The evening shadows now lay across the room, as heavy as his thick arms.

"No, she's not back yet," Grace said, holding on to her sense of humor. "That curiosity of hers is enough to kill a cat. Probably lingering somewhere on her way home, trying to satisfy it."

"She knows about curiosity and cats for sure," Wade said.

"Legendary curiosity," said Papa.

"Don't we all know it," Johnny said. "We've got the nosiest sister in the whole town."

"More like the whole state," said Jason.

"Speaking of curiosity and cats, I remember the last time we went to the river together. She told me the Minerva story," Wade said.

"The who?" asked Papa.

That spring day weeks ago, an evergreen branch from a giant sequoia swayed like a natural fan above

Wade and Amber. From the murmuring river a balmy wind blew. Beneath the tree where strawberry begonias blossomed, they sat on a cushion of crushed flowers. She unwrapped the lunch she had packed and handed him a vanilla-wafer sandwich of salami and sweet pickles.

For a while they had munched the sandwiches silently and studied the soothing colors of crimson primrose and golden alpine poppies bordering the river.

When they had crunched on the apples and nuts she had brought for dessert, they had buried their garbage and had thrown the shells toward the river. Suddenly a mouse skidded from under a clump of flowers and scurried away with a nutshell that had a little meat left in it.

"Now there's an industrious animal," Wade had said, laughing.

"How adorable he looks with his cheeks fat with the nut. Good thing no cats are around."

"Uh-huh," he answered lazily.

"Wade?" Amber's voice took on a new lilt.

He turned to her, all ears.

"Have you ever looked at the cat-and-mouse game with the mouse's eyes?"

"No," he said, "I don't have beady eyes." Then he kept silent. When she looked like she was looking, something about her face reminded him of Papa Westbrook when he was telling one of his tall tales.

"You know," she said, chewing on a blade of grass, "while the cat walks around proudly with its hunting chest stuck out saying, 'I smell a rat,' the mouse is squealing and fluttering his tail, shrieking, 'I smell a cat!' Minerva was such a mouse."

"Minerva?" said Wade.

"Now, Minerva was a fat mouse," Amber explained. "She liked to eat."

"What did she eat?"

"Spiders and creepy crawling things like grubs and caterpillars and centipedes. But she pined for the chance to get inside somebody's kitchen. She wanted to nibble on cheese. Not your ordinary American cheese; she craved cheddar cheese. Rich and tangy. A sharp cheddar cheese is what she yearned for. And although she had never before eaten this cheese, she had heard of its incomparable quality. Minerva, after all, did have impeccable taste.

"Minerva would vary her diet sometimes by eating tree bark, roots, nuts, and field seeds. These were common enough mouse foods, but then her cheese tooth would start bothering her, and she'd begin craving the more elegant cheddar, that gourmet dish for mice.

"Minerva's mother, however, was quite concerned. She had said often enough, 'Minerva, don't be meddling around People's houses.' Minerva's mother despised People and often referred to them as that disgusting, heartless human race of animals that are always trying to stamp out the whole family of mice with their poisons and traps.

"Minerva's mother was a concerned mother mouse who looked after her offspring with a discerning eye. Tried to teach Minerva mouse about the perils and pitfalls of life."

"Just like all mamas," Wade added.

"But as the old folks say, 'Children will be children.'

"One evening, I guess it was about seven o'clock, Minerva got an awful fancy for some cheddar, the deep yellow sharp variety. She ate a few grubs, but they didn't satisfy her. They weren't the right texture. They only whetted her appetite for cheese.

"Remembering her mother's earlier lessons, Minerva thought about all the reasons she should not pine for the forbidden food. First of all, she didn't want to upset her mother. Usually Minerva was an obedient daughter. Then again, she knew that to go cheese searching was a dangerous undertaking."

"Uh-huh," Wade said.

"You see," Amber said, "there were all sorts of mishaps awaiting a too adventuresome mouse. For instance, the possibility of encountering a mousetrap, that steel-jawed contraption that would gape its mouth and close its fangs on a mouse tail or a mouse toe."

"Dreadful!" Wade said.

"Yes. Thinking about it made Minerva shudder. Then there were those absolutely impossible People, who would resort to all sorts of strange behavior at the sight of a mouse. Women who screamed loud enough to burst a poor mouse's eardrums. Grown females who jumped on milk stools and held their dresses above their knees like little girls. The male People would come out and try to rescue the women doing their stool dance of fright by killing the mouse.

"Minerva's cousin, Alfredo, had been cornered, shot at with a pistol, beaten with a kitchen chair, and left for dead on top of the garbage heap.

"There were dire consequences to be considered. And the last hazard of all was that most mangy nuisance, the cat.

"Even though Minerva had never seen a cat, her mother had once described one for her."

"What did the cat look like to the mama?" Wade asked.

" 'The cat, my dear Minerva,' the mother began, 'is a mangy creature with sharp knives for claws. Indeed, one clawed paw can hold a whole mouse in its viselike clutches. What makes it even more contemptible is that it lives with that awful breed known as People.

" 'The cat has a roaring voice. The "meow" is a whining sound like a high-strung wind out of the north, pouncing down on the ears, enough to make one quite deaf.

" 'The cat,' Minerva's mother continued, 'has long stiff hairs hanging off its dreadful mouth. When it makes the high whining sound, the hairs tremble with a terrifying quiver. And it's always showing off for the People by taking advantage of helpless mice."

"How awful for the mouse," Wade said.

Amber went on with the story. " 'You never can tell what color the cat's going to be, either. Some come black as night. Others white as cotton. Some are motley-hued. Some are three-colored cats with cavernous mouths. There are huffy orange striped ones too. So don't count on an exact complexion. A cat can be any one of several colors.

" 'The tail is an instrument of deception. He swishes it from side to side. That's supposed to be a sign of contentment. Don't believe it. I've seen them swish their tails from side to side while slapping and pawing a mouse.

" 'Always beware the fat tail. It usually means the cat is vicious. Now, if you see a fat tail accompanied by hair sticking up all over the body like a moving brush with bristles, look out! That's a mean, ornery animal. Known to victimize and prey on some poor mouse.

" 'But you know you're doomed when you smell the cat's breath. It is as hot as hell. The tongue reminds you of the fires of hell. It is red. And when you see the cat's tonsils, it's all over.

" 'Now listen, Minerva, this is very important.' And the mother mouse stared the daughter mouse squarely in the eye. 'Before you see the claws, the whiskers, the color, you can smell the cat. As I have told you, his breath is hot and rank. It reminds you of stagnant pools where skunks have lingered. When you smell the cat, it is warning enough. Do not come out of hiding'—Minerva's mother pointed a cautious finger at her daughter—'for you smell a cat.' "

"The mama mouse had the situation covered," Wade said.

Amber continued. "Now Minerva had listened intently to her mother's warnings of woe about the cat, and she was appropriately terrified, but her desire for cheddar cheese ran unchecked even though, as I say, she had never tasted a piece before.

"About a week before that, her mother decided that Minerva was old enough to hear about the death of Minerva's father. He had met a fate similar to her cousin's, except it was a cat who got him. It was a cat who ate him.

"Minerva tried hard not to think about cheese. But every time she looked at the gnawed hole her father had burrowed into the People's house, she thought about a nice piece of cheese. It was an irresistible longing. And every time she saw that particular shade of deep yellow on a butterfly, on a fallen autumn leaf, on a daffodil, her mouth watered in uncontrolled drooling.

"She wanted to tell the other mice, but she was too ashamed of this compelling urge.

"One day while she was out scampering near a woodpile, she had the most extravagant yearning for cheese. No words of caution seemed to stick in her mind. Not the lesson of the claws as sharp as knives. Not the picture of the screaming women whose husbands used chairs and guns as weapons against mice. Not even the gaping horror of the steel mousetrap could quell this surging passion. The only possible answer to her great desire was a nibble, at least one nibble of cheese.''

''She was hungry for cheese, all right,'' Wade said.

Amber said, ''Now, it was late in the day, when the sycamore cast shadows from the tree branches on the house walls, and the wind had come out of his cocoon in the sky to holler down the corridors of the alleys of time. But Minerva had her urge. She became a hunter. She would have her wedge of cheese. Her morsel of gold.

''A quick glance told her that Mr. and Mrs. People were home. There were two Fords—one red, one blue—in the driveway. She could not, however, smell the cat, but she saw long gray hairs lying about. Somewhere a cat crouched.

''Minerva would not be stopped. She scampered from the woodpile and hid under a tire of the red Ford parked in the driveway.

''From where she sat curled up beneath the tire, she could more clearly see the hole her father had bored in a wall of the house. She didn't think about what had happened to her father, though. She thought only of the smell of cheddar.

''The coast looked clear. She ran across the vast open space between the car and the hole in the wall, making herself as small as possible. There was terror in each quick step she took, but the need for cheese was stronger. Before she knew it, she had come to the hole. She had second thoughts. Should she turn around and go back to her woodpile?

''A furtive movement behind her sent her scurrying into the hole in the wall.

''Inside the hole. Now she was between the outer and inner walls of the house. She found she was trembling from fright, but she had made it this far safely. She sniffed. Yes, she could smell cheese. She made herself perfectly quiet. Listened. There were People around, but they seemed to be in another part of the house.

"Minerva tiptoed to where the hole opened on the inside of the wall of the house and looked out on a shiny green linoleum floor. Her nose told her there was water about.

"She could smell some meat sizzling in an oven. She was in the kitchen then. That was good. The kitchen was where the cheese was kept.

"She took a deep breath and wheeled from her safe position behind the wall. She sniffed the delicious perfume of cheese. Then she spied it. It was right next to her.

"She rushed to the wedge of cheese, but part of it was laced with steel and wood. 'Steel,' she whispered to herself. 'This is a trap.' But some of her mice friends had told her that if a mouse was very careful, she could safely nibble a little of the cheese.

"Minerva moved adroitly and so did not spring the trap.

"She peered and saw how she could grab a bite without moving the mechanism of steel.

"She bent over and tasted the cheese. 'Scrumptious!' It was the best food she had ever tasted.

"She carefully bit off another piece. 'Ummm. Heavenly.'

"She ate more and more. The trap did not budge.

"Her little mouse stomach was almost full.

"As she was preparing to take another bite she heard a shrill scream that caused her to dig her toes into the linoleum, but the linoleum was not solid ground, was not dry land, and so instead of clinging to earth, she went skidding across the slick linoleum floor, away from the escape hole."

Wade caught his breath. "Poor mouse."

"In the distance," Amber continued, "she heard heavy, running feet.

"Now she remembered in minute detail the description her mother had painted for her of the screaming woman on the familiar stool with her dress pulled up. These, then, were the husband's footsteps she heard advancing.

"Soon he would be upon her.

"Minerva got her bearings and began to scamper back toward the hole.

"Out of nowhere she smelled a peculiar odor slap her across her face. Just as she reached the hole she saw a ball of stiff gray fur blocking her way.

"There before her hunched a steel-gray cat with flickering green lights for eyes, ready to pounce.

"Minerva came to a screeching halt on the glass-green floor again.

"Everything was in a spin. She could hear the whirring screams of the woman, like the cries of a siren in her ears. The green floor swirled under her like the sea. The husband's pounding feet had abruptly stopped.

"She was doomed. She could see the cat squinch his green eyes, the powerful cat claws reach for her, the humped back bristled with brushlike hairs. And then she looked up into the red-hell tongue of the cat. Minerva knew her life was over. She would end up like her father."

"She's done for, for sure," Wade said.

"Suddenly she heard a loud crash, a chair came whizzing by her head like a bullet, but it missed her and hit the cat. The cat, fur flying, went howling and screeching, the fat tail skinnied and drooped. The cat, now reduced to a mewling pussy, slinked away, hurt and humiliated.

"Minerva gathered her wits about her. The unfortunate cat had left the hole free.

"She flew to her escape through the hole in the wall and waited within the inner compartment. When it was safe, she fled as swiftly as she could back to her woodpile.

"There Minerva found her mother waiting, her face scowling anxiously."

"Frightened half to death, I bet," Wade said.

Amber nodded and continued, " 'My dear Minerva!' her mother cried with a trembling voice. 'You had me worried to death. What a fright I have had. Where have you been?' Then her shrewd mother eyes spied the cheese crumbs around Minerva's mouth and knew.

" 'Oh, Mother,' Minerva said, her own shaking body quieted by now, 'I have been on a wonderful adventure. I have seen the cat and I have tasted cheese.'

" 'What!? Haven't I taught you better? What possessed you?' The hasty questions came tumbling one after the other. 'How could you? It must have been h—'

" 'Heavenly,' Minerva said, thinking of the cheese, her eyes rapt with beads of joy as she giggled.

"She savored the taste of cheese still on her tongue as she revealed to her mother all the flavorful dimensions of the tangy, golden cheddar.

" 'But the cat?' Her mother sighed.

" 'Oh, my dear Mama,' Minerva said, shrugging off the hazards of the hunt, 'one cannot fully appreciate the joys of heaven unless one has suffered the horrors of hell.' "

Wade ended his rendition of Amber's cat story. Grace settled her eyes on him and said, "Some story. I must say, Wade, that doesn't help matters. It only serves to prove my earlier point. Like that mouse, Amber's too adventurous. A girl who stalks snakes. Out there alone with a gun. In the middle of earthquake weather. She could have an accident. No telling what other dangerous tricks she's got up her sleeve. I'd feel much better if I knew she was in her room reading about adventures instead of out there creating them."

"I tell you," said Papa in defense of Amber, "nothing can take the place of a real-life adventure."

David was silent.

"I'm sure Amber's all right, Mrs. Westbrook," Wade said finally. "Think I'd better get across the road. My turn to set the table for supper."

TWELVE

A few hours later Wade looked up from playing his cello to see the sheriff's car pull up to the Westbrook house.

"It's late," he whispered to himself. When he'd begun playing, it was still light. Now it was dark. "Something's wrong."

The Westbrook porch light was on. The black-and-white star-shaped insignia stamped on the car door and the dark, somber uniform Sheriff Wilson wore as he marched stiffly up to the Westbrook house were distress signals to anybody who lived on Corral Hollow Road. The sheriff only showed up when there was trouble.

Although Wade could not hear a word, he could see Grace standing in the doorway wringing her hands in her apron. Then the sheriff went inside and closed the door behind him.

Wade stared at the silent cello and bit his lip.

"Sheriff's at the Westbrooks'," he announced as he went into the kitchen and took his seat at the supper table.

"Wonder what's the matter," said his mother.

"Probably nothing," his father said.

"Probably nothing," Wade repeated.

His mind could not stay on his dinner but kept darting back to the Westbrook house.

He was startled out of his reverie by a bald, hammering knock.

His father went to the door.

Wade, glued to his seat, could overhear the conversation coming from the front of the house.

"What can I do for you, Sheriff?"

"Just want to know if you've seen the Westbrook girl. She's missing."

"Missing?"

"Didn't come home this evening."

"Sure she's not down the road visiting someplace?"

"Her mother's called everybody she could think of."

Wade's mother got up and went into the living room. Wade could not move. The voices drifted to him as though from another world. It was as though some giant wrestler had him in a vise. The giant wrestler squeezed him so tight, he paralyzed his arms and legs.

His mother spoke. "My God, it's way past dark already."

"May I talk to your boy?"

"Wade!"

Wade broke loose from the giant's grip of panic. He walked into the living room.

"Seems the Westbrook girl's missing. You seen her?"

His mouth flew open, but the invisible wrestler had set up a new match inside his stomach. A full nelson to the guts.

"No, sir. I haven't talked to her since yesterday. Right before the earthquake when we were supposed to go swimming and hunting. But after the earthquake Mrs. Westbrook wanted everybody home. And then she waved good-bye this morning when I saw her going swimming and hunting with her brothers as I was getting ready to go wrestling practice."

The sheriff scratched his head. "She never reached her house, evidently."

His father said, "Anything we can do, Sheriff, let us know."

With that the sheriff left. The family returned to the table, but everybody was too full of worry to finish eating.

As they bussed their dishes to the sink his father said, "I pray to God Amber's all right."

The vigil began.

Wade and his father went across the road to talk to David, who paced up and down, wavering between jumping in his pickup to go look for Amber and staying near Grace in case the sheriff brought back news or in case Amber herself appeared with some sensible excuse for her absence. At this point he'd even take a stupid excuse for her absence. Worry was taking the place of rage.

"Amber, where are you?" Wade whispered as he stood under her chinaberry tree. The giant panic wrestler was back, and his grip was awesome; he bent Wade's head down to his chest.

Then Wade heard the sheriff's car lurching along the road, headed back to where they all stood waiting in the Westbrook yard.

The sheriff said, "Went down to talk to the Reyes children. They hadn't seen anything unusual. Think we'd better get everybody we can to go searching."

David, now spurred on by something specific to do, dashed to his pickup with the twins. Wade heard him mumble, "Maybe she's had an accident and is lying somewhere on the side of the road, hit by a car."

Papa Westbrook looked like all the air had been let out of him. He sat next to Grace.

Wade and his father hurried across the road and hopped in their truck.

Mrs. Dewberry joined Grace and Papa Westbrook on the porch bench. A giant inkwell had splashed over the sky and snuffed out the sun. Here and there stars spotted the stained dark, and the grim-faced men in their pickups turned on their headlights and pierced the somber paper of night with high-beamed slashes as they scoured the roads that Amber might have taken.

As hours passed and the search continued, Grace's eyes seemed to sink to the back of her head, fill with water, and run over.

Her weeping was an eerie accompaniment to the odd symphony of car and truck motors and tires whining.

Finally the men reported back to the Westbrook house.

Nothing.

An avalanche of helplessness swept over David, his shoulders stooped over the phone as he dialed the doctor's number.

"Dr. Goldberg, David Westbrook here. No, it's not just my wife's migraine. I'm calling about Amber. She's missing, and my wife . . ."

David hung up the phone and went to sit by Grace, who looked grayer and grayer in her lavender, her hands trembling the way tomato vines quiver when the Tracy wind is up.

On the opposite couch Wade, the twins, and Papa shuddered.

Wade's parents stood in the doorway, helpless.

A set of squealing tires signaled new hope. But it was only the doctor with his black bag and hypodermic needle.

After Dr. Goldberg left Grace stretched out on her

bed like death, her weeping eyes now closed in drug-induced, temporary peace.

There was nothing left for anyone to do now but go in their houses and rooms and wonder, "Where is Amber?"

THIRTEEN

"Where is Amber?"

The second day of her daughter's disappearance, Grace imagined all manners of horrors.

Was Amber dead by accidental shotgun wound?

Dead by rattlesnake bite?

Assaulted by demented murderer?

Sometimes Grace was consumed by rages and shook her fists at the sky, threatening to skin Amber alive, if she was alive. But those four words—*if she is alive*—soon smothered all her anger and left only agony.

The migraines disappeared. There was no room for anything but her loss, not for headaches or back pain or colds or sore throats. Every other pain diminished in the face of this paralyzing trauma.

"Where is Amber?"

If Grace had been a photographer, she would have shot pictures of gnats swarming, hissing vipers, and the parched skin of earth just before an earthquake. She was beside herself with grim visions and totally uncentered. The cooking pots looked wrong. The gas flame never flared brightly enough for her eyes so full of darkness lately, and so meals burned.

She forgot the ratio of flour to shortening and lost the recipe for her favorite crust. The twins took cautious bites out of each serving of apple cobbler and lay their forks down.

David ate only to sustain himself and so paid scant attention to biscuits hard as rocks, burned beans, and scorched rice.

Papa Westbrook stared off into space from time to time and whistled to himself, "Sacred Mountain, Sacred Tree, Sacred River That Runs to the Sea" in a minor key at the dinner table, where it was totally inappropriate.

Across the road evening was falling in the Dewberry living room. A bougainvillaea sunset fringed with crimson flames spread its fire through the plate-glass window by which the cello was stationed, and then went out.

Wade sat down to play the cello.

First he rubbed the catgut bow hairs with the sticky rosin until they were tacky enough.

He massaged the bow until he remembered how water sparkled like jewels in the tight curls of Amber's black lamb's-wool hair when she surfaced after diving.

He had sat down to play the cello.

Before starting, he tightened the pegs. His strong fingers turned the wooden knobs until he created from memory Amber's flute fingers strumming mountains, trees, and rivers into being. He worked until the wires sang in tune.

He had sat down to play the cello.

Before he could begin, he oiled the ebony fingerboard, the spruce belly, the maple scroll, the graceful body.

He polished until he was dizzy with Amber's hips, the curve of her legs dripping with beads of water, her swimsuit clinging as she stepped out of the river.

He had sat down to play the cello.

But the bow was quiet.

He remembered that the fingers pulling the shotgun trigger and whipping the snake's tail belonged to the same hands that called forth notes from the flute. And the sweet sound of her voice telling about the curious Minerva mouse was the voice with the *who?* cry caught in its throat, describing the Priscilla Redwine baby. And everywhere he looked, and especially when he looked at his cello, he saw her.

He had sat down to play the cello.

Quest

FOURTEEN

Amber followed the path of the river deep into the forest. The weight of the heavy backpack slowed her down as she walked through ferns and over fallen trees.

In the backpack she carred a knife, soap, toothbrush, matches, a few cooking utensils, a sleeping bag, gown, jeans, socks, shirt, and underwear. Her swimsuit was folded up in her back pocket, and she toted her gun across her chest.

Beyond these things, she carried questions and the need to know, strewn like bright pine branches balanced on top of the backpack.

"Why didn't they tell me I was not theirs?" she asked the air.

"Why did cousin Abyssinia abandon me? I mean, my real mother, Abyssinia, abandon me? Mother? But what about Mama? Oh, it's all mixed up." She just wanted to get someplace and think. Although there had been plenty of talk about the relatives in Ponca City, Oklahoma, the name Abyssinia was just one of the kin. Amber had never even seen her.

When she got near that part of the river that dipped into the sea, a golden eagle spread his wings, casting a long shadow over her path. And when she stopped at the place where she had decided to camp, the eagle sat down on the tree like an animal vacationer at a human zoo and stared at her, his long talons wrapped around a eucalyptus branch. He did not move his powerful wings for an hour as he watched her claim her place in the woods.

When she had finished unpacking, the mist came down and lifted the eagle up from the eucalyptus to the hills and carried him far beyond the mountains.

She looked all around her at the pine and sequoias swaying in the breeze, the fragrant bushes of sage and rosemary, the red-blushed clouds half an hour before sunset.

Her backpack no longer weighed her down. She was ready to go walking; walking is when she did some of her best thinking. She needed to think and walk during these last minutes of dusk.

She started off in the gathering twilight, moving away from the river, taking in the seascape of a wild tangerine sun plunging toward the violet and scallop-waved ocean. Now she kept hiking and looking up, naming the wheeling and perching birds, discerning their songs, their feathers. Did they have any answers, these innocent birds?

She looked at the blue jay who passes truth to her baby birdies by instinct and asked, "Blue jay in the sequoia, can you tell me why they hid the truth from me?"

"Brown wren above the pine, why?"

"Robin in the evergreen, why?"

"Thrush in the bunchberry bush, why, why?"

Then some sixth sense directed her eyes to the ground, and her heart thumped up in her throat and hung there.

A mass of crawling creatures writhed and wriggled before her feet.

She could not get around them.

She heard something fall thudding to the ground behind her. She could not go back, either.

They blocked her path. Raised their dangerous heads and swayed their hooded eyes at her.

Mama snakes, daddy snakes, and baby snakes dressed up in their diamond backs and glittering scales.

The hackles on her neck rose and her muscles locked.

The creepers set up a clatter of rattling.

"Oh, Mama," and Grace's warnings came back to haunt her, "Snakes are out there, Amber."

Why, oh why had she laughed at her mother?

But she's not your mother, the snakes seemed to say.

They rattled in front of her. They rattled behind her.

Why had she laughed at her mama, who was scared stupid of snakes, who couldn't even stand to look at a worm.

I tell you, she's not your mama, the snakes mocked.

Some part of her was aware of clefts and abysses in the customary wood sounds. Chirpless birds. The crickets in the tall grass had stopped cricketing.

The dry rattling mesmerized the whole forest until it made dumb every other sound.

Nearest her, one snake licked his hot tongue at her; fangs shot out like a flickering fork of fire.

Whose child are you? You're not your mother's daughter. Not your daddy's girl. Not your brothers' sister. You don't know. You're ignorant!

Instinctively she jumped high and grabbed a tree branch, hoisted herself up, and swung her feet over the limb out of the way of the family of snakes.

Her breath had left her body and was still crouching in the middle of the swarming serpents.

Just when she was about to retrieve her breath she

heard a hiss. She looked above her and spied a grandfather snake wrapped around a thick branch. He looked about nine feet long and three feet thick.

Ignorant. Ignorant. Ignorant. Not your mama's girl.

She fell backward out of the tree into a clump of bushes away from the snakes and started running.

"Snakes, get out of my way. My way. My way. My way." She was her own hollering echo.

She ran and ran. Somehow she got back to the campsite.

She was shaking so, she had to sit down and hold her head in her hands.

After a while she could hear the sounds of the forest again.

The birds were chirping. The crickets singing. She removed her head from her hands and listened intently, but she could not hear any rattling.

She started whistling. At first the whistling came with hardly any breath in it. Without any tune anywhere near it. A halting sound. Her skipping heartbeat began to steady itself as she half whistled on. By the time the whistle became as clear as a whistle should be, her pulse had gentled itself and night had wrapped a soft black cloak around her.

She knew that if she had started exploring a half hour later, she would not have seen the nest of snakes. It would have been too dark.

She dared not venture out again unless it was to go back home.

Home.

She rolled her sleeping bag up and put it in her backpack but quickly took it out again.

Home? *You're an outcast. Abandoned. A daughter under false pretenses.*

Besides, she wasn't letting any snakes make her go

back home. Besides, it was too dark. But when she thought about the rattling snake nest, she wasn't too sure. Maybe when morning came . . . It was pitch black. She could hardly make out the river and the sea. Besides, where was home?

She unzipped the sleeping bag and settled down. Was it fear of the dangers she had walked into or a blinding anger that she had been abandoned and lied to all these years that infected her eyes and made her cry? After a while tiredness swept all other considerations away, and she fell sound asleep.

In her dreams she heard sharp bird talons and saw a beak striking again and again against yellow-and-black flesh, slippery-skinned and fanged with poison.

Soon after the strange dream, the morning sun climbed to the edge of the earth and hesitated.

She woke up itching and scratching. *I've been snake-bitten,* she thought. But when she looked down at her skin, she saw that she was covered with a fine rash.

"Poison ivy," she moaned.

As she sat up in the sleeping bag the bright sun showed her the poison vines tangled among the innocent mint and sage.

The rash broke out in whelped stings over her face, arms, hands, and stomach where she had scratched during the night.

She made a poultice of mint and mud, but still the fire of the poison ivy taunted her fingers with promises that if they only scratched a little, they could put out the fire, but whenever her nails dug into her skin, the poison fire smirked and spread its stinging torture even more.

She stopped scratching and thought of a fire for tea; this thought exaggerated the itching. But she gritted her teeth, told her fingers to be still, and went to fetch water from the river.

Where the water dipped into the sea, she saw the blue color of it begin to change. The water sparkled brightest here and began to churn itself from light blue into indigo fringed with white foam until the water flowed clear indigo. She saw stones at the bottom of the river and little schools of fish flashing in and around the stones as they wiggled through the crystal stream. The sight of the water made her more thirsty. She leaned over and dipped the pan into the indigo blue.

On the way back to her small camp she saw the eagle bent over a long, looping serpent. Then he lifted the rattler in his claws and climbed the sky.

So one of the snakes had stalked her and slinked around, ready to poison her, but the eagle had watched and swooped down and made the preyer the preyed-upon.

"Well, that's the end of snake worry," she said as she gathered kindling and dead wood for the fire "with an eagle like that watching."

For tea she picked wild mint leaves and slipped them in the pot of water. For breakfast she found the spotted brown eggs of pheasants.

For lunch she caught a perch, seasoned him with sage, and smoked him over her fire.

For dinner she ate dandelion greens, the roots of cattails, which tasted like white potatoes, and juicy blackberries whose dark sweetness dribbled their syrup down her chin. She saved a few berries to rub on her skin as a repellent to the mosquitos.

At day's end she settled down and listened to the river at the spot just before it poured into the sea. The incense of evergreen enchanted the forest, while the eagle beat his wings against the twilight sky, soaring until the holiness of mountain, river, and tree disappeared and only the image of the eagle remained on the retina of her eye.

Before turning in for the evening, she took a soothing bath in the river. The fire of the poison ivy was beginning to smother itself by now.

As she dipped and ducked, soaping herself, she remembered other dips she had taken with Wade and her brothers. A scavenger of shame sank its crabby claws in her heart: she was remembering the betrayal and the symphony of the snake. *Whose child are you? You're not your mother's daughter. Not your daddy's girl. Not your brothers' sister. You don't know. You're ignorant!*

FIFTEEN

At last the sound of water lulled her to sleep, and she dreamed of the ocean and her place under the trees so intently, she imagined she was a water drop merging with a drop of pine sap. Then, turning, she welded herself to herself. Her breasts first. Then her spine, into one long, rippling cord until she was almost whole. A marbled miracle.

When she was brown, shot with gold, an emerging jewel snuggling the seed of herself deep into the lining of her mother's watermelon belly, when she curled herself into a prenatal ball, when she had done all this, she felt the power of herself.

Her ears opened like seashells. All during her centuries of nine months, the loudest whisper she ever heard was this: *Yes, yes, and yes.* Laughter, and always the whisper: *Yes, yes, and yes.*

The yeses now and then took on new form, and she was visited by the most extraordinary music coming down to her water home—an intricate, embellished voice rich in notes but with the echo of music sung through water. Somebody was singing just to her, in a voice as sweet as a flute. And she dreamed the song of herself.

It was while she was listening to the coda of the song that she almost discovered the thing that she knew she did not know. Some truth so ancient, so basic, it was as though some part of her had always known it. Voices. A woman's. A man's. But the husky voice was not David's and the first voice was not Grace's. Both like talking music. Maybe the male and female voices of God?

Later, when she had walked through the fire that singed her naval after she had come up out of the water, she saw faces too vague to discern. The faces of . . . They were bending over looking at her. Just when she thought she had their faces almost clear, they wept and turned their heads. Then, like two kites escaping out of sight beyond a tree or over a hill, a strong wind snagged them, lifted them up higher, and turned their heads away from water.

Her eyes searched for them, but her sight could not hold them. They did not look back at her but stepped like leaves into the mouth of the wind.

SIXTEEN

Two days passed and Amber was no closer to understanding that most baffling puzzle. What happened? Why was she abandoned? Then she thought about the dream. Were the people in her dream her cousin Abyssinia, her mother-cousin Abyssinia, her father-cousin Carl Lee?

To herself she said, "If I am not my mother's child, my daddy's daughter, grandpa's Amber, the sister of twins, then who am I?"

She thought and thought. She collected free corn. She fished and smoked catches of bony perch and spiny bass. But still no answer.

If she could just have her flute. Maybe it would help her think.

Search for answers through the medium of music, an inner voice seemed to say.

How to do that?

With the flute, it answered.

"But the flute is home," she said.

The voice was still.

She would sneak home when everybody was asleep and get the flute out and come back to the woods.

But the snakes—she could only go home when it was daylight.

She could do it; wasn't she always the first one up? The rest would still be sleeping if she went early enough.

At the first blush of dawn she started out. When she reached home, the house slept the deep sleep of ignorance, unaware of her presence.

It only took her a minute and she was gone again. She played the flute, with the sound of birds composing in the background. With tumbling water splashing between notes. With the wind in the pines haunting her breath breaks.

She played all day, stopping only to eat. And the flute, too, seemed to ask why, one thought with her mind.

She played and played; she played the sun out of the sky, she played until her lips would no longer quiver. And she passed out in her sleeping bag, the flute tucked in beside her like a baby. Down and down into the softest sleep.

In her dream she heard a flute playing high rondos and lilting minuets all around her forest bed. She lifted her head from her midnight dreams, perked her ears, and listened.

The soaring notes beckoned her. She unzipped her sleeping bag, threw the top cover aside, and stood up.

A ribbon of sound pulled her.

Whose child are you, out here alone and alone? the flute seemed to say.

There across the moonlit path, there in a clearing of fallen logs covered by a wild rambling of bougainvillaea blossoms, she saw a sight that made her gasp.

A troupe of deer—does, bucks, and fawns—stared at her with wide velvet eyes.

One taller than the rest, with antlers like a crown, held a silver flute in his hand. "Come, my Amber," he said in a voice as smooth as an oboe. "You love music and you love knowing. Come, and I'll play you your answers."

Her nightgown flowing behind her like a veil in the

wind, she slipped down the path toward the buck until she stood among the purple flowers a few feet away from the deer.

She was so close, she reached out and touched a fawn. His whole body trembled under her gentle strokes.

Then the tall one motioned her to a nearby log.

When she was comfortably seated, he lifted the flute to his lips. And the music came, sprinkling awe everywhere. For a moment the wind did not blow. Even the moon turned her head and listened with a silvery smile playing around her moon mouth.

A mother is the one who loves you.

A sterling sound flew from the flute. It lingered on the pine needles and tumbled into the flowing water, then drifted away on the churning foam where the blue became indigo.

A daddy is the one who cares.

Soon the sound lifted itself from the river and the sea, and returned riding on the back of the wind.

A brother is a dear rascal, a bother you cannot do without.

When the music came circling back, the deer began to move.

First in rows of threes.

Then they paired off and skipped into an intricate ballet of steps. Their hooves touched the ground and rose up. The fawns galloped in the middle, hooking hooves in hooves. Graceful in their spotted coats dappled with moonbeams.

Amber had never seen such prancing choreography, and neither, evidently, had the flowers. For all around her the bougainvillaea leaned breathless color toward the dancing deer and blushed with rouged petals of excitement.

When the music and the dance reached pure rapture, the handsome deer nodded his antlers.

And Amber stood up.

The sound of the flute pulled her away from the blushing flowers and in among the deer.

Her feet floated beneath her. And she touched each animal as she circled the dance forest floor.

The wind blew a steady hum through the pine trees while the deer backed away to let her dance alone in the center of the clearing.

And the flute-playing buck trilled a seamless sound, without pauses for breath.

And she danced on and on, weaving in and out of the circle of deer.

Soon the high music dropped from the top of the pines and sequoias and drifted down around her feet and settled on the forest floor.

When the music stopped, she found herself kneeling before the crowned deer.

When she looked up again, the forest was clear. The animals had gone. But when she looked down, she saw patterns of hoofprints in the dirt and grass.

The dawn woke her up. Her spirit soared. As she unzipped her slipping bag new music played in her head.

She remembered the lyrics and what they declared:

A mother is the one who loves you
A daddy is the one who cares
A brother is a dear rascal, a bother you cannot
do without

SEVENTEEN

It was the third day and she was exhausted. Her spirit was happy. A window had been lit in her mind, and when the truth hit it, it sparkled and sparkled. Yet the energy it cost to light the window, the all-day-long and into-the-evening playing of the flute, cost her.

On this third morning she rested and thought and thought. Now she was not so angry with her parents who had raised her but toward the ones who had left and abandoned her; she wasn't sure how she felt. That would come later.

"I'm going home," she said. And home to her was Grace and David, the twins, and Wade.

At the water's edge she brushed her teeth. The stones in the water seemed to reach under her lids and paint her eyes with the morning gold of legends. And the sound of the waves washing over the sand and stones was the sound of water speaking.

It was as though these three days had opened a spiritual place in her mind, and she was open to night and day dreaming. Ready to receive the speech of deer and water. And this morning the water spoke to her.

The water said, "I am the smell of sweet decay. The current of old order, established before man made his footprints in the sand near the sea. The river knows. The river knows about fish and about man. I was there when man swam with fins, when his skin was silver scales. When he lost them and stepped out of the sea. When his skin was all colors and he owned everything his eyes could see. I am the dark smell of life. When the river flows briskly, its water is as murky as mud. They say water changes everything it touches. Even metal will wear down when troubled by water. Hill and mountain. Given time, water will erode rock into sand. And when I wish it, I move to music. I swell to music, and sometimes I rage, intrude upon the land, swirl, churn, surge, and roar. Now and then I cry acutely, shroud myself in fog and grieve.

"Now I know music. I have washed stone for thousands of years and tasted sulfur in my mouth. Now I know music and the river aroma of eternity. I am water and I know everything."

"You say you know everything," Amber said. "Then tell me about the Indians."

"I will tell you about the earthquake."

"Yes."

"One day long, long ago, the earthquake who lives beneath the river, just where I dip into the sea, became lonely and decided he would venture out of the water and onto dry land to see what wonders the earth held.

"But in order to come up, he had to break through rocks beneath the sea. Then through the crust of the earth until he was swimming up to the waves. When he got there, he walked on the sea until he reached dry land.

"The people ran when the earthquake came toward them. Even the rocks, steady as they had always been, were shaking with fright. The mountains, long known for their courage, trembled at the sight of the earthquake coming out of the water.

"The earthquake was so happy to touch the shore, he skipped under the valley, danced through the insides of the mountains. Touched roads and unzipped the dark fabric of the earth.

"Now, the earthquake was dressed in clear red. If you were a tree or a rock or a mountain, you could see his stately presence. If, however, you were a mere human being, you could not imagine his appearance. You could only feel his presence by the way his movements shook everything in sight. By watching a rock, a tree, a mountain, you could feel him moving through everything.

"Even though the earthquake was huge and looming and large, he was innocently ignorant of his capabilities and effect. So what if the earth trembled beneath his feet? What does a human feel when he stomps his giant feet across the ground the ant is crawling on? Nothing. So it was with the earthquake. He was so immense, he did not appreciate his largeness in respect to the rest of the world. He was. And that was sufficient reason to do what he was supposed to do. An earthquake quakes in much the same way that a storm cloud storms. Because it has to. Surely the gray cloud does not care who it whips with vicious downpours stippled with thunderbolts, whether man-killing sharks or openmouthed babes, it goes about its business of storming.

"The earthquake was about its business of quaking.

"But there was one group of humans who were not afraid of the earthquake. The Indians. When the earthquake quaked, they offered up a ritual dance. A presentation of praise and welcome. A bright dance at once joyful and hospitable. They made fires. Feasted. And danced until they were dizzy. And all around the celebration the mountains moved and bounced. The rocks pranced. The trees wiggled and joined in the jubilee. It turned out that the mountains, rocks, and trees only needed someone to show them how to appreciate the earthquake. The earthquake laughed and felt like a high celebrity in the midst of these festive folks.

"And then, at the very height of the celebration, the Indians were cut down by an enemy tribe. The earthquake began to cry when he saw the hearts of his friends pierced by weapons. Their tepees destroyed, their feasting pots bubbling with food overturned, their lifeless bodies strewn all over the countryside. The slaughter took a century, but to the large earthquake whose sense of time was different, it seemed like a day.

"He went back to the water. He went back to where the river dipped into the thirsty sea. He cried so hard, his tears mingled with the river's until a mighty flood came. After he had cried out all his sorrow, he fell asleep. And he slept for years. But whenever he wakes up, he thinks about his Indian friends and begins to pace up and down the river until he squeezes rocks in the palms of his hands, knocks the interior apart, and comes up through the earth's core. He swims up from the river bottom, strokes his way onto the land, and begins to stomp up and down the earth, frightening every creature in sight. Uprooting permanence.

"Defying order." The water ended her legend.

Amber sighed.

"Then tell me about myself," she said.

"You are the girl of many mothers," the water said, then spoke no more.

"What?" said Amber.

But the water had finished talking.

"Well, anyway," said Amber, "I'm going home. Right now."

Quenched

EIGHTEEN

On the third day Wade saw Mrs. Westbrook waving him over, and he hurried across the road.

"I can't find Amber's flute," she said. The usual air of lavender that traditionally sealed itself around her was absent, making her seem less herself.

"What do you mean?" asked Wade.

"It's not there. You know she kept it in her bedroom just beside the dresser. I went in to dust her room this morning, and it's gone!"

"Gone?" said Wade, thunderstruck. "Are you sure Mr. Westbrook or one of the twins or Papa Westbrook didn't move it?"

"I asked them," she said. There were both tears and laughter in her voice.

"The flute."

"Wade . . ."

He looked at Mrs. Westbrook, and he couldn't breathe. "Excuse me," he said. He flew across the road.

His cello stared at him in its usual place in front of the living room window.

The flute melodies that had made him toss and turn in his sleep during the early dawn—had he dreamed them or not? "Sacred Mountain" flute sounds had drifted in through the curtains.

Something squeezed his heart, and this time it wasn't the phantom wrestler of panic.

Out of the living room window he saw Sheriff Wilson drive up in the Westbrook driveway.

When the sheriff pulled away, Wade saw Mrs. Westbrook go out to her garden to water the lavender.

Just then his mother came into the room and stood next to him, also watching Grace tend her garden.

"Why, that's the first time I've seen Grace in that garden since . . ." his mother said.

Wade looked at his cello.

Then he turned to his mother. "Mama," he said, "I'm going for a walk."

He heard music coming from the river, closer and closer; the sound grew. He walked toward the sound, a ribbon of melody pulling him toward it. There was another sound. The sea. He was following the river to the sea. And the magnetic tug of the combination of music and sea was irresistible.

He heard the flute, but it was not played like a flute. It was played like a bow and arrow. "Sacred Mountain, Sacred Tree, Sacred River that Runs to the Sea."

He followed the trail of notes, a river of sound, through the path by the water. It had been a long time since he had been this close to the sea.

He brushed aside hanging branches, stepped over feathery ferns, walked through needles of light lacing through the trees.

Now the notes were more crystal, more urgent, more near. And all around him he saw trees reaching so high, they threatened to scrape the sky. Music so tall, it could create light and stars and full moons.

A doe and her speckled fawns gamboled across his path unhurried, as though they were used to seeing only friendly creatures this far in the woods.

Then he spotted her walking toward him, her backpack in place, her lips on the flute, a long kinky ponytail tied almost neatly, so he knew it hung in a question-mark curve down her back.

He stood still.

She saw him.

She pulled the flute from her lips. She was all grace and sureness. A cinnamon face of sparkling ebony eyes and a splash of white, white teeth.

When she reached him, they clung to each other.

"Amber, Amber, Amber," he said. Mirth ran out of him like a laugh locked up too long.

"How could you leave?"

"I had to."

"Why?"

"First I have to tell you about the attic."

"The attic?"

"What I discovered there. You see, I'm not who you think I am or who I thought I was. I'm not my mother's and father's child. When I was a baby, I was abandoned. I'm not Johnny and Jason's sister." And she went on to describe to him the contents of the letter from Abyssinia and Carl Lee.

"You were adopted?"

"Something like that. And I'm not my grandpa's Amber."

"And nobody ever told you? That's mean!"

"I thought so. At first."

"And now?"

"Now I don't know. I had these dreams about my folks and everything bothering me lately. Earthquakes, Indians, what my folks mean . . . The dream . . . Part of the dream was the legend of the earthquake who lives in the river. Nobody had ever told it to me before in full detail."

"No, come to think of it, I've never heard it explained. But tell me, Amber, how can you dream a legend?"

"I can't tell you how. I just did."

"But wait. Tell me the dream about you and your folks. Did it explain your birth?"

"In a way. The water spoke. 'I am the daughter of many mothers.' " And she tried to imitate the female voice of water.

They walked hand in hand now. Going home.

Before long, the sea was far behind them and only the river and the trees were left.

And then suddenly the earth trembled.

Earthquake!

Above their heads the giant pines wagged back and forth.

Then all of a sudden, pine needles and pinecones started raining through the air, and the evergreen and troubled fragrance of the tall sequoia trunks swayed dizzily all around them.

Through the lace-light of quivering trees they started running as fast as they could. Alongside the river as it flowed tumbling toward the sea, they scrambled.

They fled toward home, moving frantically as the trees rustled and bent all around them, their cones flying through the air like shingled baseballs.

"What an earthquake!" she gasped, breathless with hurry. "When I have children, I will not let them play cowboys and Indians if the Indians are always the villains."

"What?" said Wade.

"I'll explain later," she said.

The earthquake roared.

"Is it going away?" asked Wade, trying to gauge the trembling of the ground as he ran.

"Perhaps it's just started."

They looked into the water as they skirted the swelling, complaining waves. The river spoke in an ancient language. Now out of breath, they tiptoed past it like eavesdroppers. The wind began to rise. And it sang.

When the river began to answer the wind more violently, and the earth shook more powerfully beneath their feet, they crept along, silently praying each step of the way.

Finally they reached Bear River Road.

"We've made it this far. Won't be long before we're home," she said.

They kept pushing on toward home as the earthquake quaked, and the eagle dipped his shadow away from the sea, then led them on.

Already Amber could imagine herself sitting in the living room on the round blue trumpet-vine rug, her brothers on both sides of her, her parents sinking themselves in the palm of the purple couch, her father rubbing the couch's shoulder with one hand and holding her mother's hand with the other. When the smell of lavender cut the air like incense, that's when she would tell them how much she loved them and why she ran away. Then they would tell her the whys of her birth, and her grandfather would wisely nod his head in agreement with Amber's right to know. She could hardly wait.

"Home," said Amber, so softly that Wade had to strain his ears to hear, her fingers tightly laced in his, so close. So near to the magic of love and water and eagle and home. So close to home.

JOYCE CAROL THOMAS is a lecturer, a writer and producer of four plays, and an accomplished poet with three published volumes to her credit. She is the editor of *Ambrosia,* a black woman's newsletter, and a Visiting Scholar at Stanford University. Currently she makes her home in Berkeley, California.